TALES FROM THE WEEKEND

TALES FROM THE WEEKEND

Edited by
David J Howe

First published in 2017 by Telos Publishing,
5A Church Road, Shortlands, Bromley, Kent
BR2 0HP, United Kingdom.

www.telos.co.uk

ISBN: 978-1-84583-120-2

Contents

THE ROAD TO HOLLY TREE FARM

Paul Lewis

Jacob did not have to look outside to tell the weather had taken a turn for the worst. Wind whistled through the hairline gaps around the window, jiggling the curtains, and the temperature in the living room had dropped sharply, leaving it chilly and damp. The old boiler was trying its best to keep the place warm but was losing the battle.

Not for the first time that evening Jacob frowned at his watch. Sarah was cutting it fine. If she left it much longer, and if the snow turned from light flurries to the full-on blizzard the forecast had threatened, she might be left struggling to make it home.

Today of all days she had to meet up with her old mates for Christmas shopping in Cardiff. Jacob had implored her to call it off but she was having none of it. She always looked forward to their annual reunion, this year more than ever after the upheaval of the move. Against his better judgement, Jacob had eventually given in.

To be fair, Sarah was a good driver. But she wasn't

used to the country roads yet, didn't know them like he did, had no inkling how treacherous they became when conditions turned bad; the council gritting lorries didn't venture this far up into the hills.

Yet as dangerous as those winding country roads could be, they were nothing compared to the road to Holly Tree Farm.

Jacob laughed grimly. *Road.* Bit grand for something that was little more than a dirt track, pocked with deep holes that resisted all efforts to repair them. Worse yet, a steep bank fell away to one side, dropping sharply to the dry stone wall that marked their boundary with their neighbour's farm. If the track iced over …

No. He did not want to think about that.

He realised he was pacing the room and sat heavily on the sofa, putting his mobile phone within easy reach on the cushion next to him. He tried to relax but the fluttering nerves in his stomach would not let him. Sure, he'd been annoyed with Sarah for going out and spending money she did not really need to spend on frivolities when they really needed to spend it on the old farmhouse. But he would forgive her that, he'd forgive her anything, as long as she made it home in one piece.

He was just thinking about calling her when his mobile rang, making him start. Jacob snatched it up. *Sarah,* the screen informed him. 'Thank Christ,' he muttered as he thumbed the green phone motif to take the call. 'Sarah? Where are you?'

The signal was appalling, scratchy with static. '*Jake?*'

She sounded so distant it was like she was calling from the other side of the world. Even so, he caught the hitch in her voice and realised she was deeply upset. '*Jake?*'

He lunged up off the sofa and began walking the room in anxious paces. 'Sarah, love. What is it? What's wrong?'

'*Jake … I … I crashed the car.*'

'What?' He shivered as the last remaining heat in the room suddenly drained away. Fluttering nerves solidified into a kick in the guts, tempered only slightly by the realisation that she must have been okay or else she couldn't have called. 'Listen, just calm down, okay? Now … where are you?'

'*Oh, Jake, I crashed the car,*' she said, as if she had not heard him. '*On the road …*' Static drowned her out. '*… farm.*'

'Sarah!' His hand hurt and he realised he was clutching the phone tightly enough to make the plastic casing creak. He relaxed his grip, telling himself he had to keep a level head for both their sakes. 'Sarah, just tell me where you are. I'll come and get you.'

'*… hit my head … hurts … so bad …*'

The words faded away, which could be because the signal had broken up or because Sarah had slipped into unconsciousness.

Concussion, he thought, and the cottage walls seemed to close in on him. Even if she was close enough for him to reach her without too much delay, he might need to get her to hospital. And the nearest hospital was thirty miles away, on the other side of the Brecon Beacons, with a blizzard about to do its worst. With luck he could probably just about manage the journey if he had to – assuming their aging Clio was not so badly damaged it was beyond being driven.

'Stay inside the car,' he said, practically pleading with her. 'Just stay in the car. I'll come to you. Do you hear me, Sarah?'

Silence. He tried calling her back. Nothing. Jacob glared briefly at his mobile, as if it holding it personally responsible for this entire bloody mess, then hurried into the kitchen. It had been impossible to hear her clearly but he was fairly certain she was trying to say she'd crashed on the track leading to the farm. At most it was a twenty-minute hike from the house to the main road. Hopefully she was closer to the cottage than that.

His stomach churned. He felt sick. As he pulled on his boots, his mind was awhirl with possibilities, none of them pleasant. For the first time he regretted the fact that they only had one car. But fixing up the house had swallowed their savings, and as they taught in the same school it wasn't like they needed two for work.

He grabbed his North Face coat from the hook on the back door and zipped it up with trembling fingers. After slipping the mobile into one of the pockets he reached for the torch he kept by the window; power cuts were hardly a rarity in this part of Wales. He hauled the door open and had only just stepped outside when the howling wind wrenched it shut behind him. Without bothering to lock it, Jacob set off into the night.

It had not been a working farm for years so there was no expensive machinery to steal but he'd left the security lights on anyway. He always did when Sarah was out at night. Although she would never admit it, he knew she was afraid of the dark. Now, though, their intensity emphasised the absolute blackness beyond their reach. They also drove home to him how heavily the snow was falling. Fat flakes swirled frantically in the twin cones of light as the wind stampeded down the valley, roaring like a mighty beast.

Jacob shivered and pulled up his collar, thumbing the torch switch as he hurried away from the farmhouse. The beam was ineffective in the face of the blizzard, only powerful enough to illuminate the track a few paces ahead of him. He did his best to keep to the right, away from the steep slope, but with the track twisting and turning he could never be sure of his bearings.

His heart skipped a beat when he felt the phone vibrate in his pocket. The wind gusted so furiously he could not hear it ring. Getting the mobile out was a struggle; his fingers were already numb with cold and he cursed himself for forgetting his gloves.

Finally, he managed to extricate it. The screen was bright but so obscured by whirling eddies of snow that he had to hold it a few inches from his face to make out the caller ID. *Sarah.*

'Honey, don't panic, okay?' He had to shout to make his voice heard above the wind, which seemed determined to snatch the words away as he spoke them. 'I'm on my way. I'll be with you as soon as I can.'

'*Jake … Christ, Jake, there's something outside.*'

He pressed the phone hard against his ear. 'What?'

'*Something's outside the car, Jake … huge …*' He swore loudly as the signal broke up again. '*… can see it … oh god, Jake, I'm so scared …*' More fucking static. Jacob wanted to lash out, punch something, anything, in frustration. Without thinking he picked up his pace, the phone still jammed against his ear, his chest beginning to ache from exertion and the cold air he was gulping down into his lungs.

'Sarah! Sarah, can you hear me?'

'*… monstrous … blocking out the stars …*' Her voice suddenly rose into a distorted shriek. '*… trying … get inside. Jake, help me, oh dear god, please help me …*'

The phone suddenly went dead. Jacob had never felt so helpless, or as wretchedly useless as he did right then. Her words made no sense at all. Something huge enough to block out the stars? The biggest thing they'd seen since moving here was the bull their neighbour hired to service the herd on his dairy farm.

Then he remembered her once telling him about a recurring childhood dream. About monsters chasing her in the dark. It used to wake her up screaming, she'd said, and they had laughed at the ridiculousness of it. But if she'd smacked her head the old dream could have resurfaced, only with concussion making it seem real to her.

For a moment he could have sworn he heard something roar in the distance, and immediately dismissed it as the bellowing of the gale. Now he was spooking himself, he thought angrily.

He struggled on as fast as he dared, leaning into the wind, eyes streaming so heavily he had to wipe them every few seconds to have any chance of seeing where he was going and even then the road ahead was little more than a monochrome smear.

The snow was not just cold but painful with it, driving into his face like icy needles. Although the torch was useless he kept it on anyway, drawing comfort from it even while its light perceptibly dimmed as the batteries started to fail.

When the phone rang again he had no time to say anything before her hysterical voice was shrieking into his ear. '*… can't stay in the car, Jake … smashed the windscreen trying to get in … trapped if I stay here …*'

'Don't,' he screamed. 'I swear to god, Sarah, there's nothing there!'

Again there was no indication she had heard him, her voice so strident with terror he would have struggled to make out her words even without the static. '*… going … lose it in the woods …*'

'Sarah, listen,' he used his best teacher's voice to try to get through to her. 'Don't leave the car. It's just concussion, Sarah. Remember that dream you used to have, about the monsters?'

Nothing.

'Sarah?' he bellowed, but the screen was dark.

He stuffed the phone back into his jacket and began to run. He ran until it felt like the air had turned to shards of ice in his chest. He could not think beyond the need to find her before she did anything stupid, like leaving the warmth of the car in a blizzard to escape some horror that existed only within the confines of her injured head.

When he did find the car he almost ran past it.

The Clio had plunged down the bank, coming to rest against the dry stone wall with its bonnet concertinaed. One headlamp was out but the other was working otherwise the car would have been invisible. Jake stood there, gasping for breath. He'd lost all sense of distance and had no idea how close or far away the woods were.

There, he thought, with a sob of relief when he saw the deeper darkness of the woodland at the far end of the field beyond the wall. Then he glimpsed something huge move across the field towards the tree line. Just the snow, he told himself, just the snow and the wind and his anxiety making him see what could not possibly be there.

There was no time for stupid fantasies. He had to get over the wall and into the woods if he was to stand any chance of catching up with Sarah before exposure set in. As he scrambled and slid down the slope towards the Clio he became aware of the stench of petrol and switched off the torch; it was too dim to see by anyway.

He hadn't intended stopping to check the damage to the car. Sarah's life was far more important to him than anything else in the world, least of all a rusting heap of metal. But as he scrambled past the wreckage he caught glimpse of something from the corner of his eye that made him stumble to a halt.

Slowly, trembling, he reached for the driver's door.

Opened it.

Sarah was wedged upright in the seat, pinned into place by the steering wheel, force of impact having rammed it deep into her chest. Her lolling head was angled unnaturally towards him. There was just enough reflected light from the headlamp for him to see her eyes were wide open and her face was dark with blood.

Jacob moaned and backed away, shaking his head wildly.

Yet even as grief turned his brain as numb as his hands, he instinctively recognised there was something wrong.

Something that made no sense at all.

Sarah had died on impact. No doubt about that.

And yet she couldn't have. Because if she had …

From inside his jacket pocket, the phone began to ring.

PAUL LEWIS has written hundreds of comedy sketches for UK television, including *Spitting Image* and Hale & Pace, as well as radio sitcoms and plays. Paul has collaborated with Steve Lockley on several novellas and short stories, many of which are collected in *The Winter Hunt and Other Stories*. His solo stories have appeared in numerous anthologies and magazines and he is the author of fantasy novel *The Savage Knight*, published in 2011, and *Small Ghosts*, a novella to be published by Telos Moonrise in 2017. He works as a senior communications officer with the NHS in Wales.

AN AFFAIR OF THE NIGHT

Darren Shan

Liz Carr was weeding the small garden in front of her house when the vampire attacked. The sun was setting – a warm, red evening – and she was concentrating on the weeds, squinting to find them in the dusk, determined to finish the job before night. Suddenly, two hands snaked around her waist and yanked her up into the air. A pair of lips fastened on her throat. As she opened her mouth wide to scream, her assailant growled throatily: 'If you don't keep quiet — I'll give you a hickey!'

'Gavner!' Liz shrieked, shaking her head free, spinning in his arms, kissing him passionately.

'Pleased to see me?' the vampire called Gavner Purl grinned when she came up for air.

'Stupid question!' she grunted, kissing him again. Then, finding the ground with her feet, she took hold of his hands, left the weeds for another day, and dragged Gavner inside.

Later that night, they lay stretched out before a burning fire, talking softly, hugging and kissing. It had been three years since Gavner's last visit, and they'd a lot to catch up on. Liz told Gavner all about her work – she was a nurse in a nearby hospital – and he in turn told her of his exploits as a Vampire General. His stories sometimes chilled her – part of his job was finding and executing rogue vampires – but this time he had nothing unpleasant to report. They'd been a busy but unremarkable three years — no killings.

As Liz studied Gavner's scarred face and dark rimmed eyes, she found herself recalling their first encounter twenty-six years ago. She'd been a young woman, a mere twenty-three years old, while Gavner (though she didn't know it at the time) was more than eighty.

She ran into him in St Matthew's hospital, where she'd started a few months earlier. She was on the late shift, working from midnight through to the early hours of the morning. It was a quiet time, most of the patients asleep, no visitors, the corridors deserted. Liz liked it. She'd always been a bit of a loner, and she enjoyed doing her rounds alone, no distractions, with only herself for company.

She'd just checked on an elderly patient, and was coming out of his room, when she heard harsh breathing in the hallway. Glancing up, she saw a burly man propped against a wall, staring at her with dark, unfriendly eyes.

'Who are you?' she snapped, clutching her clipboard close to her chest, as though it would protect her if the stranger attacked. 'What are you doing here?'

'I need … blood,' the man gasped, then slid down the wall to a sitting position.

Liz thought about calling security, but then the man groaned feebly and her nursing instincts took over.

Rushing to him, she saw that he was bleeding from a wound in his stomach. His face was white and creased with pain. She faltered at the sight of his scarred features and blood-specked jumper – she knew intuitively that not all the blood was his – but only momentarily. Seconds later she was kneeling over him, examining his wound, looking for a compress to staunch the flow of blood.

'Hold this in place,' she said, pressing a large wad of napkins over the hole in the man's stomach. 'I'll go get a doctor.'

'No!' the man hissed, grabbing her before she could leave. 'No … doctors!'

'I have to!' she snapped, trying to wrench free. 'You'll die otherwise.'

'No,' he insisted stubbornly, and something in his voice made her pause. 'All I need is … blood. Get me blood. I'll take care … of the rest.'

Liz started to object, but as she stared into his eyes, her mouth closed and she said nothing. 'Blood,' the man whispered softly, widening his eyes, piercing her with his gaze. 'Bring me blood. Don't tell anyone. No doctors.'

'OK,' Liz sighed, rising. As she walked to fetch the blood, she realized the man had somehow, in some way, hypnotised her. She thought she could break free of his spell if she tried hard — but she didn't bother. As menacing as he looked, she sensed no harm in the stranger, and believed the best thing would be to do as he asked and give him some blood.

When she returned with two plastic bags filled with a sloshing red liquid, the man tore them from her hands, ripped them open and drank from them like a wild animal, greedily gulping the blood down, moaning with pleasure. Finished, he rested his head against the wall a while, then bent over and dribbled spit around the wound in his stomach. Rubbing the spit in, he spat on the wound again, then again. As Liz watched incredulously, the blood stopped flowing and the wound scabbed over.

'How are you doing that?' she gasped.

'My spit has remarkable ... healing powers,' the man wheezed, leaning his head against the wall again, smiling painfully.

'What happened to you?' Liz asked.

'Had a run-in ... with a group of men ... who didn't like my face,' the man chuckled, then raised a rough, bloody hand. 'Gavner Purl,' he said.

'Liz Carr,' Liz replied, taking his hand and shaking it. 'I'm a nurse,' she added unnecessarily.

The man grinned broadly. 'I'm a vampire — pleased to ... meetcha!'

'What are you thinking about?' Gavner asked. The room had gone very quiet and Liz realized neither of them had said anything for several minutes.

'I was remembering the first time we met,' she said, sitting up and running a hand through her long, light brown hair.

'*That* was one for the books,' Gavner laughed, tickling her gently. 'I never understood why you trusted me so readily. You even brought me back here once you'd patched me up — knowing I was a vampire!'

'I didn't really believe you were a vampire,' Liz smiled, 'not to begin with. I thought you were confused — or mad.'

'But bringing a stranger home ... That was dangerous. And silly. There's no telling what I could have done.'

It was true. When the man claiming to be a vampire rose and stumbled for the exit after a few minutes' rest, Liz had stopped him. 'You can't leave,' she said. 'You're in no state to go anywhere. Stay. There are spare beds. I'll put you in one and –'

'No!' Gavner grunted, lurching towards the door. 'Can't stop. Can't let medics … examine me. If my enemies learn … my whereabouts, I'm … dead.'

'Then come home with me!' Liz pleaded, the words popping out before she had a chance to consider them. 'I have a small house several miles away, in the countryside. I live alone. I'll look after you until you're better.'

Gavner paused at the door and stared back at her. 'You don't mean that,' he whispered. 'You can't.'

'I do,' she insisted, stepping up beside him.

'But … you know nothing about me. I crawl in here … in the dead of night … covered in blood … tell you I'm a vampire … and you want to take me home?!? Are you crazy?'

'Maybe,' Liz smiled. 'But you'd be crazy too, to turn down such an offer. Now — are you coming or not?' She held out a firm hand.

Gavner gazed silently at the fingers, then chuckled and slipped his own large fingers around them. 'Guess I am,' he sighed, and let her lead him out of the hospital and into the safety of the night.

Liz called in sick that morning, and stayed home with Gavner. The two went to bed, where they slept the day away. Liz woke before the vampire in the afternoon and spent a few hours pottering around the house, waiting for him to wake. When he finally yawned, stretched and rolled out of bed, he smiled at her sheepishly. 'Sorry if my snoring kept you awake,' he said. It was a familiar greeting of his, one he'd used for many years, since she first complained of his bear-like snores.

'That's OK,' Liz smiled, pecking his lips. 'I slept like a baby.' Her nose wrinkled. 'Speaking of which, you <u>smell</u> like a baby — with a dirty nappy!'

Gavner laughed guiltily. 'I washed in a stream three or four nights ago, but I haven't had a chance since then.'

'In that case, the first order of the night is to get you straight into the bath,' Liz said, leading him to the bathroom.

'And afterwards?' Gavner asked innocently. 'Any idea what we can do to pass a long and otherwise dull night?'

'Oh,' Liz replied with a fond smirk, 'I'm sure we'll think of something ...'

The next few nights were delightful. They always were when Gavner returned from his work as a Vampire General. They cooked elaborate meals, drank expensive wine, danced to old records which Liz had inherited from her mother, and spoke at great length about their lives.

Gavner had more to say than Liz, of course, since he was almost a hundred and ten years old. He'd seen more of the world and met more fascinating people than she ever would. She loved listening to his tales of the past, encounters he'd had with famous or interesting figures of history.

'You were really friends with Groucho Marx?' she asked.

'Sure. He used to say I was the greatest bloodsucker

he knew — except for his lawyers!'

Liz still felt uneasy about Gavner's need for blood. She knew he only took small amounts when he drank, never harming those he fed from, but it seemed ghoulish to her. They didn't discuss it much.

It had taken Liz a long time to accept Gavner's vampire claim. As he recovered in her house and gradually told her of his true nature, she thought he was making it up. When she realised he was serious, she feared for his sanity and considered reporting him to the proper authorities. It was only when he sat outside with her for a few hours one day, and started to burn, that she began to think there might be something to his supernatural tales.

He stayed with her for almost a fortnight that first time, regaining his strength, hiding from his enemies (she later learned that they were a small group of vampire hunters, men who'd tracked Gavner through twelve different countries, hunting him for sport). There was no romance — they simply became good friends. When he left, she was sad to see him go, but not overly so.

A year later, he returned one cold night, bringing roses (he stole them from a cemetery), to thank her properly for her kindness. He'd stayed more than two weeks this time, and their friendship developed into something deeper and more meaningful. Since then, Gavner had spent as much time with Liz as his duties permitted. Sometimes he dropped in three or four times a year, for weeks on end; on other occasions two or three years would pass without contact. Liz always worried about him when he was absent – knowing he could die any time, and she'd never hear about it – but Gavner did nothing to assuage her fears.

'If I phoned or wrote letters, it'd only make you think about me more,' he said when she pressed him on the subject. 'I'm a creature of the night — you're not. Our lives are too different to ever fit together neatly. Let's cherish the moments we share — and try not to think about each other when we're apart.'

She'd sometimes thought of becoming part of his world – if he'd blooded her, she could have explored the night with him, as an equal – but Liz didn't want to become a vampire, and Gavner never asked her to abandon her humanity for him —his was a hard life, and he didn't wish it on her.

And so they'd continued for twenty-six years, on-and-off lovers, united by the night, divided by the day.

Liz prepared breakfast (vampires called their first meal of the night breakfast), while Gavner shaved in the bathroom. The vampire normally didn't shave very often, but his bristles were extremely tough and irritated Liz's skin, so she made him lather up and shave them off every night when he stayed with her.

While she scrambled eggs, she found herself studying her reflection in the mirror on the shelf near the cooker. She was forty-nine years old, and though she'd aged well, there was no denying the traces of time evident in the lines around her eyes, the grey hairs at her temple, the dry skin around her throat. Liz Carr was getting old — that didn't worry her; but Gavner had hardly aged during the quarter of a century she'd known him — and that had been gnawing away at her for most of the last decade.

'Admiring yourself again?' Gavner murmured, sneaking up behind her and kissing her neck.

'There's a lot to admire,' Liz grinned.

'There certainly is,' Gavner agreed, then dipped his fingers in the saucepan and scooped some egg into his mouth.

'Wait your turn!' Liz snapped, slapping his fingers with her fork.

'I'm hungry,' he complained, sliding away from her, licking his lips.

'No wonder,' Liz snorted. 'You get more exercise snoring than most people get jogging!' She lifted the saucepan from its ring and emptied the eggs on to a pair of matching plates.

'That's always the way,' Gavner sighed. 'When I first arrive, my snoring doesn't bother you and you cling to me tightly. By the time I leave, you can't stand it and are ecstatic to be rid of me!'

'I guess love deafens me for a while — but only a while,' Liz laughed. Then, as she handed Gavner his plate, her features softened and she said quietly, 'Will you be leaving soon?'

Gavner nodded, tucking into his eggs. 'Tomorrow. I have to go to Vampire Mountain — we're having our great Council in a few months.'

'Another Council?' Liz tutted. 'You almost died trying to get to the one before last. I don't know why you bother.'

'Tradition,' Gavner smirked. He stuck his left foot out and wriggled the three toes on it at her — he'd lost the other two twenty-four years ago, on his way to the Council she'd referred to.

'You'll be gone for quite a while then,' Liz said, staring down at her food, not touching it.

'A few months to get there, two or three months in the mountain, another month or two to return. I'll try and drop in on the way back.'

'So this is our final night together,' Liz noted.

'For a while,' Gavner agreed. He paused. 'Are you OK? You seem a bit down.'

'I'm fine,' Liz smiled thinly. 'Just sad at the thought of you going.'

'It won't be for long,' Gavner reassured her. Six months — maybe less. I'll be back before you know it.'

'I'm sure you will,' Liz said, then smiled firmly. 'Hurry up and eat your eggs. I want to make the most of our last few hours together.'

'That's what I like,' Gavner chuckled, wolfing down the last of his food. 'A woman who knows her mind …'

The sun had set when Gavner awoke. 'Sorry if my snoring …' he began to mumble, then stopped when he realized Liz wasn't there. Stretching, he scratched under an armpit and sighed happily. She was probably outside, tending to the garden, or else she'd popped into town to buy some supplies. He'd cook a meal for her, have it ready when she walked in. Their last meal of this visit. It would have to be something special, something she loved.

Gavner was thinking hard about the food when he walked into the kitchen and saw the parcel and card on the table. He frowned, strode to the table and studied the objects with suspicion. The parcel was small, carefully wrapped in Christmas wrapping paper, with a label attached, on which was penned: 'For you — the love of my life.' The card was standing upright, half open, and he could glimpse Liz's handwriting inside.

He knew instantly that something was wrong, and it was more than a minute before he reached out, picked up the card, opened it, and read:

'Gavner, my love — it's over. There's no easy way to put it. I've been thinking about it for months – no, *years* – and I haven't been able to come up with a more artful way of phrasing it. So I'll say it again, as plainly as before — it's over.

'These twenty-six years have been magical, my love. You've enriched my life in wonderful ways. There have been disappointments – I wish we could have been together all the time, and that we could have had children – but I won't remember those when I think about our relationship in the lonely years to come — I'll recall only the great times, the nights you held me close, the amazing stories you graced me with, the love we shared which has given meaning to my life (and, I believe, yours).

'So — why the dramatic farewell? It's simple — I'm getting old. I don't think you've seen that yet – in your eyes I'm as young as I was when we first met – but it wouldn't be long before you did. In another five or six years, I'll be in my mid-fifties, but you'll still look like a man in his early thirties (albeit one who's had a hell of a rough ride through life!).

'I don't want you to see me growing old, Gavner. If you were ageing too, it would be different – we could wrinkle together, and take comfort in each other's fading glory – but you aren't. You're a young man, and will be for many decades –centuries! – to come, long after my body's crumbled and my spirit's passed on.

'This is the right time to call it quits, while I'm in my (almost!) prime, while our love's as strong as it's ever been, before I grow old and spoil it all. I can't bear the thought of having you around when I'm stooped with age and preparing for death — too messy; too painful. It will be hard for you, I know - and just as hard for me - but it's the right thing to do. I'm convinced of that.

'You'll see that too, I think, but not straightaway. You don't leap to conclusions as quickly as I do — I guess because you've got so much more time than me to weigh up all the various options. If I'd discussed this with you, face-to-face, you might have talked me round to your way of thinking, and convinced me to stay and let you back into my life — and that would be wrong. If we don't break now, sharply and cleanly, we never will — and our lives will be all the more painful because of it.

'So I'm going, my love. I'm leaving. I won't return to the house until you've left for Vampire Mountain — and don't try to trick me by pretending to go, then doubling back, because I'll know! When I do return, it will only be to gather my belongings and sell off the house. I'll move to another town - maybe another country - and start afresh. You never know — I might even find a new man to share my final years with! (I'm open to any sort of man, *except* vampires — one of those per life is enough for any woman!)

'I'm weeping as I write this, my love, and this is only the start of the waterworks — I might be wailing for years to come! But I know in my heart I'm doing the right thing. What we've shared was beautiful, but now it must end and we must go our separate ways — back to our own worlds.

'I've left a little present for you. You'll hate it, I'm sure — which is why I picked it! I'd much rather you winced every time you looked upon my gift and thought of me, than burst into tears. Make good use of my gift, Gavner — and thank your lucky stars every time you gaze upon it that you got rid of me when you did, before I kitted you out with any other monstrous designs!!!

'Anyway (big sigh!), I could go on forever (and ever and ever), but what's the point? I love you and always will (even if I find some other man to grow old with), and I wouldn't swap any of our nights together for all the glories of this world or any other. But the time has come to part — so part we must. I hope we meet again in Paradise or Heaven, or wherever it is mismatched lovers go when they die — but not any time soon!

'A toast, my darling vampire: to long lives (yours will be longer than mine, of course!), lots of luck — and a universe of love.

'Goodbye, Gavner. I love you.

'Liz.'

Gavner read the message twice. Three times. Four. On the fifth occasion he stopped halfway through, laid the card down, and picked up Liz's parting present. He was cold inside, colder than he'd ever been, and although his head was full of desperate thoughts - that he'd run after her, find her, and wipe these foolish ideas from her mind – on a deeper level he knew that he'd never see her again, that she'd made her decision and it was his duty to respect it.

He turned the parcel around several times, delaying the moment when he had to open it, wishing she'd waltz through the door, yell 'Fooled ya!' and kiss him like she had so many times before. When that didn't happen, he finally ripped the paper off the present, shook it free of the last few strips, and held it up to the light.

Boxer shorts. Bright yellow. With tiny pink elephants stitched into the lining.

'You've got to be kidding!' he gasped aloud. These were awful! The most deplorable, loud, ridiculous shorts he'd ever seen! If she thought he was going to wear these, she must be –

He stopped, recalled her line in the letter about wanting him to wince every time he gazed upon her farewell present, rather than sob. A weak smile flickered across his lips, and he knew he'd wear the boxers, wear them until they fell to shreds. And though he'd think of Liz every time he pulled them on or off, he'd have to smile at the memory of the ghastly present, and as great as his sense of loss would be, he'd be able to bear it.

'Nice one, Liz,' he grunted, turning the shorts around, grimacing as he spotted more pink elephants on the back. Balling the shorts up, he read through the message one final time, then unballed the shorts and studied them again, running a rough, scarred fingertip over one of the tiny, smiling, pink elephants.

And then the Vampire General clutched the shorts to his chest, perched against the table, closed his eyes, whispered her name – 'Liz!' – and began to slowly and lonesomely cry

DARREN SHAN was born in London but is Irish and lives with his wife and young son in a small village in Limerick where he has resided since the age of six. Darren studied Sociology and English at Roehampton University in London. He then worked for a cable television company, before setting up as a full-time writer.

Darren's breakthrough came with the publication of *Cirque Du Freak* in January 2000. He has now published close to fifty books, both for children and adults (the most recent adult novels have been released under the name of Darren Dash). *Cirque Du Freak* has been adapted into a (faithful) manga and a (rather less faithful) movie, and his books have sold twenty-five million copies worldwide. His books are on sale in 39 countries, in 31 languages. He has made bestseller charts in America, Britain, Hungary, Ireland, Japan, the Netherlands, Norway, Taiwan, the United Arab Emirates, and other countries.

A big film buff, Darren also reads lots of comics and books. Other interests include art, football, pop and rock music, going to live gigs and theatre, roller coasters and travel.

BACK AT SIX

Freda Warrington

'I'm not happy about this,' said Lucy. Her blue eyes were full of the low-burning hostility he'd grown to dread. The look broke him, every time. 'You know how easily he gets overtired. Where are you taking him, exactly?'

Graham spoke softly, so the boy wouldn't hear. 'The place you and I used to go. He'll love it.' He forced a smile, trying to make peace. 'We've been through this. You already know exactly where we're going, and exactly what time I'll bring him home.'

Lucy took a step back, broke eye contact, nodded. She looked at their son: six years old, teasing the dog in the back of the car and oblivious to their conversation. 'Okay. Sorry. We both have to learn to work around this, don't we? Have fun. Don't forget to give Truffle some water. And don't let him eat anything disgusting. The dog, I mean.'

A small joke? They shared a wary laugh.

'Anyway,' she said, still smiling. 'This is about Tim, not us.'

Graham strode to his car, made sure Tim was strapped in and reversed off Lucy's drive before she found a new reason to delay the outing. *You're wrong*, he thought. *It is about us.*

Half an hour later, he and his son were strolling along a forest path. Tim talked non-stop. School, football, computer games – an endless tangled stream of enthusiasm. Truffle, a ginger-coated mongrel of mostly terrier blood, raced back and forth after scents, wild with the excitement of discovery. Such simple pleasures. *Oh, to be a small boy*, thought Graham, *or a dog*.

Had Lucy's eyes softened when they'd laughed together?

Perhaps. Just for that moment, she'd forgotten to be cold towards him.

Graham had parked in Grinley Woods car park, unloaded the cool bag and slung it over his shoulder, with the picnic rug on top. How familiar, this path through the green oaks, holly and beech trees: he remembered the way as if he and Lucy had walked it only yesterday. In fact it had been eight years ago, long before Tim's birth. If he shut his eyes, he could feel Lucy at his side. He pictured the idyllic clearing that they'd made their own special place. A bower of sunlit green grass, wildflowers, butterflies …

'Dad, what does "No fly-tipping" mean?'

Tim, running ahead, had stopped at the edge of the clearing. Beyond the sign, defying its threat of prosecution, lay a heap of fridges and filthy sofas, builders' rubble, empty cement sacks, tangles of rusty barbed wire, torn bin bags spilling their unspeakable contents.

Graham stood with his mouth agape as if someone had punched him. Truffle ploughed on, but Tim was fast enough to grab his pet's collar and hold him back before he dived straight into the foul heap.

Quick thinking, thought Graham. *Smart boy*. Then, *Filthy irresponsible bastards!*

He scratched the back of his own neck, felt sweat there.

'*That* is fly-tipping,' he said, pointing. 'Dumping rubbish where it shouldn't be.'

'Didn't they see the sign?' Tim was indignant. His innocent outrage made Graham even more furious with the culprits. *Everything good gets ruined*, he thought. How easily the past was defiled. A shiver went over his skin, a mixture of disappointment and impotent anger. Pain shot from his shoulder into his head: an unwelcome return of the tension headache he'd been fighting all morning.

'I expect they saw it. They just didn't care.'

'Why?'

'Some people are bad and stupid, Tim. Come on, we'll find somewhere else. Put Truffle's lead on, so he doesn't get into anything he shouldn't.'

They retraced their steps a few yards. Graham scouted along different paths for what seemed an hour, losing his sense of direction. Now he saw litter everywhere. Beer cans, crisp packets, dog poop bags that had been tied up and hung on tree branches. What was the sense in doing that?

They came to a stream, turned left and walked along the bank. Bare earth, stones, tree roots. Empty coke bottles. He tried to concentrate on the murmur of water and the distant tapping of a woodpecker.

'I wish Mum was with us.' Tim paused to throw a pebble into the stream.

'So do I, mate,' said Graham. 'Maybe she'll come with us next time. Today it's just you and me.'

'But why?'

'Well … your mum and I aren't getting on very well at the moment.'

'I know, but *why?*'

'Sometimes grown-ups fall out.' He took a breath to

explain more, but a midge shot down his throat. All he could do was cough while tears ran from his eyes. By the time he'd swallowed the bug, Tim was fifty yards ahead.

Graham didn't recognise this part of the wood at all. The trees grew tall and thick. Nowhere looked like an inviting place for their picnic. Still, the woods couldn't go on forever …

Maybe she'll come with us next time.

'I'm hungry,' said the boy, turning and waiting for him. A birth defect, a slight curve in Tim's spine, meant he couldn't walk too far. He'd try: he'd keep pace with Truffle as if he could run all day, then drop with sudden exhaustion because he hadn't yet learned to pace himself.

Don't let him get over-excited, Lucy had warned.

Tendrils of anxiety wormed through Graham's chest. This was the first time he'd been allowed to take their son out alone since they'd split three years ago. He suppressed his bitterness that she didn't trust him. Trust had to be earned. He was on trial.

Not that she had any reason to distrust him with Tim. He loved his son more than his own life, and she knew it. But that wasn't the issue. She was still hurt, and he didn't know how to put things right. Operation Win Back Lucy meant that he'd swallow his own feelings and do everything her way. Prove himself the perfect father. Prove she could rely on him, in every possible way, until she let her shields down.

They still loved each other. That was the trouble.

'Dad, look.'

The stream bent right and dipped under a dry stone wall. Beyond the wall was a small meadow. It looked unpromising: rough and lumpy, full of ragwort, thistles, nettles. On three sides the green space was encircled by Grinley Woods, while the fourth side sloped away, carrying the stream towards open farmland.

The late September sun was strong, burning moisture off the grass. First hot day after a week of rain. The meadow was a sun-trap, bright and hot after the cool gloom of the trees. At least there was no litter that he could see. No signs of activity at all, human or animal. The heat lay so heavy that even the insects were still.

Graham had a sickening sense of unease. His head throbbed. Surely Tim deserved better than this. *Should have organised a theme park visit with his schoolmates. Cinema. Paintballing. A trip to Disneyland Paris. Anything but an old-fashioned picnic in a weed patch.*

He was ready to suggest they went back, but he dared not admit he was lost. Besides, he couldn't take Tim home without feeding him first. He wouldn't risk the boy going woozy with hunger. Couldn't admit failure.

'This is perfect,' he said out loud.

It'll have to do, he thought.

Tim hung back, frowning a bit, looking pale.

'Come on, I'll help you over,' said his father. 'We'll be eating in a few minutes' time. We're going to have fun, okay?'

'I forgot to bring my football,' Tim said forlornly. Then he held up a filthy yellow tennis ball. 'I found this, though!'

'Oh,' said Graham. 'Okay.'

Graham popped Tim over the wall first, then passed him the cool bag and the blanket. Truffle's jumping skills were poor, so he hefted the wriggling mutt to the other side. He wasn't a great fan of the terrier-beast, as he secretly called Truffle, but Tim adored him and that was what mattered. Graham climbed over last, scraping his hands and calves on the jagged stones. Too late, he saw a weather-worn sign from the corner of his eye. *Private. No*

Trespassing.

Damn, I hope there isn't a farmer with a shotgun around, he thought. *But who's going to see us? We'll only be here an hour or two.*

He checked his watch. Half-past two. Needed an hour to find their way back to the car – depending on how lost they were – plus half an hour to drive back to Lucy's, plus fifteen minutes to arrive admirably early. So … they had until four-fifteen. Graham was determined to make a good impression on her.

'Ew, Dad, *mud,*' said Tim. 'My trainers are wet. Look, they're filthy!'

Lucy would give Graham a black mark for that. He must take Tim back clean, happy and safe, or their first father-son outing would be their last.

'Try to keep off the muddy bits, then. Walk on the grass and don't step in any rabbit holes.'

'How far are we going?'

On the far side, the ground pushed up into a small hump with a flattish top. Maybe a remnant of medieval farming. It looked familiar. An odd wave of *déjà vu* went over him and his vision filled with sparks. He recognised the symptoms of a migraine aura; he suffered these attacks about four times a year, but it had to happen today. Great. For Tim's sake, he had to pretend he was fine.

'There,' said Graham. 'With luck, it'll be dry on top.'

Brightening, Tim let Truffle off the lead and they raced towards the mound.

Tim was in jeans and sweatshirt, fortunately for him. Graham had come out in his khaki hiking shorts and short-sleeved shirt. Nettles stroked his bare calves with a burning rash. Brambles snagged his hands. But as long as he was the one sustaining injuries, not his son, he didn't care.

To win her back. To get her away from her stupid lump of a 'boyfriend' – she didn't love *him* – and to be a family again: that was all Graham wanted in the world.

He trembled, so anxious was he to deliver Tim back to Lucy in one piece. Hot and cold waves flashed over him. Pain settled in his left eye.

They had been happy once, and he'd blown it. Usual story. Lucy, wrapped up with their young son. Graham at a teaching conference, giving in to stupid temptation with a work colleague … It had only happened once, but Lucy had found out. Once was all it took to break their hearts.

They weren't bad people. They were ordinary. He taught music, she was a doctor in general practice. Neither of them was abusive or psychopathic or even moody. He wasn't angry with her for not forgiving him, even after three years; why should she forgive him? They'd had a soul-deep bond, and he was the one who'd broken it.

Now they lived separately. She shared a modest house with the 'boyfriend'. Graham spent his leisure time looking at the walls of his studio flat, working out ways to melt through the ice-wall of his wife's pain.

He had betrayed her. He could never undo what he'd done, but if only he could patch over it, build a bridge to the future …

Suddenly he was certain that he and Lucy *had* found this meadow before. His eerie *déjà vu* was more than migraine. He looked around, visualising the landscape under heavy rain … Hadn't they come here with the history club once? They'd met through that club. So many happy days spent hiking, excavating, exploring together … until Graham had ruined everything.

'Dad, look at us!'

Tim and Truffle were jumping about on top of the

knoll. Graham smiled. No point dwelling on the past. Today the sun was shining on his face and Lucy had let him take Tim out for the first time in three years … He didn't care about nettle rash, scratches or headaches. He laughed and saluted his son, who was celebrating on top of the mound, shouting, 'I'm the king of the castle!'

When the food came out, so did the wasps.

Man, boy and dog sat in a triangle on the tartan rug. From the cool bag in the centre, Graham unpacked Tupperware containers, bottled water, paper plates, a dog bowl. Enclosing them on three sides lay the thick dark curve of Grinley Woods. In front lay a gorgeous view of fields and hedgerows. The only sign of human life was a distant wind turbine.

'Don't hit the wasps!' said Graham. Gently he wafted the pests away with a plastic box lid. 'If you make them mad, they'll sting. And if you kill them, their mates will smell the blood and swarm in to take revenge.'

'Really?' Tim's eyes went round. 'Do wasps have blood? I'm not scared of them anyway. They're just a nuisance.'

'That's all they are,' said Graham, pleased by his son's bravery.

'I wish mum was here,' Tim said again. He grabbed a cupcake before Graham could say, 'Wait, sandwiches first!'

Doesn't matter, he thought. *I might get points for being a fun dad rather than a bossy parent.*

Tim added, 'And Steve.'

Steve was the 'boyfriend.' Graham always put inverted commas around him, because he needed to believe that Steve was temporary.

'You like Steve, do you?' Graham said carefully. The

look of the thick yellow icing made him feel sick. Green lights gyrated in his vision. Some evil imp kept hitting him in the temple with a small vicious hammer.

Tim shrugged. 'He's okay. He's good for playing football with. But you're better for talking and jokes and stuff.'

'Good for that, am I?'

'Anyway, you're my *dad*. Steve's just a man that mum likes. He'll never be my dad.'

He went quiet, his mouth stuffed full of cake and icing.

Graham felt unexpected tightness in his throat. Tim was a wonderful boy, loving and funny and (usually) well-behaved. But even if he'd been the worst rascal on the planet, his father would not have loved him any less. Graham looked at the array of food and his stomach turned. He hadn't brought his painkillers. A sip of water would have to do.

This headache was down to pure stress. His entire future hung on proving himself a good parent, minute by minute. He knew Lucy wanted Tim to have his real father in his life.

Win back Lucy and Steve would simply fade away.

Unnatural movement near his son's mouth caught his attention … He saw the feelers of a wasp, exploring the underside of the cake half an inch from Tim's lips…

Graham lurched forward and swiped the cake from his hand. Tim made no sound. He stared at his father, mouth open with shock. The wasp flew in a loop and landed on the boy's sticky lower lip.

Tim's eyes widened as the insect made its slow exploration.

'Don't move.' Graham switched into calm teacher mode. 'Keep absolutely still.'

'*Ah*.' Tim was trying to say, '*Dad!*' without moving his

lips.

Was the boy allergic to stings? Graham couldn't recall any incidents. Lucy had never said … Surely, if there was a danger of their child suffering anaphylactic shock, a picnic was the last thing she would allow … But still, he ought to *know*.

Time stopped. Graham went so dizzy that his ears rang. All that existed in the world was the wasp, with its curved stripy abdomen and tiny sting poised on his son's lip …

He blinked. Time shifted. The migraine, briefly forgotten, came back like a spear through his skull. The wasp had departed and Tim was now stuffing a sausage roll into his mouth as if nothing had happened.

Graham wondered if he'd blacked out for a moment from sheer terror, or if he'd simply hallucinated the worst thing that could happen.

'Why are you staring at me?' Tim mumbled through half-chewed pastry. 'It's gone, didn't you see it fly off? Truffle, stop it!'

The terrier-beast insistently pushed his nose over Tim's raised elbow, sniffing.

'Get off! No begging.' The boy tore off a bit of sausage meat and flung it away. Truffle raced down the knoll in search of the morsel, vanishing into the tangle of weeds and long grass below. Tim giggled.

'You shouldn't feed him. It only makes him beg more.' Graham sighed, sat back on the rug with his knees raised. His legs were red-raw with nettle rash. Headache pain trickled like ice water through his neck muscles. 'I should have told Lucy not to pack anything sweet. Mind you, *we* always forgot there would be wasps. Every single time.'

'You threw my cake away.'

'But I saved you from eating the dreaded wasp!'

Tim laughed. 'Are there any more? Cakes, I mean.'

'You can have mine. Go on, get stuck in.'

Graham tipped back his head and looked up at the blue sky. He shivered. He shouldn't be cold in this heat, but migraines always made him feel like death. His head throbbed and he wanted to scoop up his son and rush him away from this place, take him home. Back at the flat they could watch a film or play computer games and Tim would be safe …

'Where's Truffle?' Tim's voice startled him. 'Truffle! Come here, boy!'

Graham found himself lying flat and suspected he'd fallen asleep.

'How long's he been gone?'

'I don't know. *Ages*. At least ten minutes.'

'Oh, lord, he'd better not have found his way back into the woods. Give me a bit of sausage roll and I'll tempt him back.'

Tim put his fingers to his lips. 'I ate them both.'

'You seem to have eaten almost everything.' Graham checked the boxes: there was half a cheese sandwich left. Wasps and flies crawled over fragments of icing in the cake box.

'Sorry, Dad. I asked if you wanted anything but you just snored.'

Damn, I really was asleep. Graham cursed himself for inattention. 'It's a good job Truffle's crazy for cheese.'

Graham rose to his feet, scanning every direction for the damned dog. Lucy and Tim doted on their pet. He'd been so focused on Tim, it hadn't struck him that losing Truffle would be an almost equal disaster.

Then the ginger head appeared, ears flapping. Truffle had something in his mouth. A grey flat object. He heard Lucy's voice, *Don't let him eat anything disgusting*.

'Drop it.' Graham took two strides and seized the dog by his collar before he could turn and run off again. What in God's name had he picked up? Graham gripped the object's edge, but Truffle dug his teeth in, growling. They played tug-of-war. Great fun for Truffle, perhaps.

Not a stone. Something softish. Leather? No, some kind of metal.

Lead.

'Truffle, *drop it!*'

The mutt dipped his head and let the item drop onto the grass. Definitely a piece of lead, dull and flat and ragged round the edges. Christ, how much lead did it take to poison a dog? What if he'd swallowed part of it?

Graham seized a plastic water bottle, got hold of Truffle and forced his jaws open. He trickled water onto the lolling tongue. Truffle thought this was a great game and began snapping at the stream of water, tail wagging.

'What are you doing?' Tim said, excited.

'Washing his mouth out. God knows what he's eaten.'

'Let me!'

Tim spun in circles with the bottle and Truffle pranced after him, catching the water in his jaws, lapping, spraying it everywhere. Wonderful fun for them both. Tim's laughter and Truffle's joyous yips grew deafening. Graham sank down onto the grass, light-headed with relief that they were enjoying themselves, that the dog wasn't lost after all.

If Truffle fell sick later … Lucy wouldn't necessarily blame him, would she? She didn't need to know about the scrap of lead. He quivered with feverish chills. This outing had been one long panic attack. But to see his son laughing … worth every moment.

He picked up the object and wiped off the dog-slobber with a napkin.

Not a fragment of roof flashing, as he'd thought. It was old. A few inches square, bent, the edges corroded, covered in scratched characters.

Thanks to the history lectures he and Lucy used to love, he knew what it was.

The letters scratched into the metal were Latin. A curse. He knew the sort of things these tablets usually said: *To the bastard who stole my cloak from the baths. May he freeze naked! Septimus, the old goat who would marry my mother – let his bits shrivel and drop off. He who betrayed my beloved sister – betray him in turn, O blessed goddess.*

But he was no expert. This, he couldn't translate at all. He sat up, catching his breath. The letters danced, rising off the surface like a holographic illusion. He wanted to tell someone – but there was only Tim, too busy playing with his pet to be interested. If only Lucy were here … He held an imaginary conversation with her in his head.

'Look at this! A Roman curse tablet. There must be an old ruined temple under here. That's what the mound is: the remains of a temple!'

She would be so excited. He envisioned what lay beneath: perhaps a mosaic floor with an image of the particular deity they'd worshipped here. The gaps in the walls would be stuffed full of similar tablets. Prayers, curses. Lucy would start to make plans. They would talk of bringing the history club here. They would contact the archaeologist who'd given the lecture. Organise an official dig …

But wait, hadn't they been here once before?

Déjà vu again.

That's why the rough green patch felt so familiar. The weather had been poor that day, Graham recalled, steel-grey and drizzling. They'd approached from a different direction, across the fields rather than through the woods.

He remembered that a couple of people had taken one look at the knoll and hurried away. Their unexplained departure cast unease on the rest of the group. Then a friend of theirs – a retired teacher in her sixties – had felt faint. They'd helped her to sit down. She had remained on the edge of the mound with her head in her hands for ten minutes, murmuring to herself,

'There's something bad here. Something really bad. Can't you feel it?'

The other five had stood around, unsure what to do. At that point, a man had come up from the farm and started arguing with the group leader. The leader swore he'd got permission from the farmer, but the farm worker insisted that they were trespassing and must leave at once or shotguns would be deployed.

Well, it was easy enough for a group to scare itself. Any group of teenagers could give themselves nightmares in a dark old house, or playing with a Ouija board. That sort of primal terror was highly infectious. Mid-quarrel, the clouds had collapsed under their own weight and unleashed a massive downpour of rain. End of argument. Heavy curtains of water drove the group downhill, over the stream, through the flooded fields and back to their cars mired in the farmyard ...

Tim uttered the dreaded words: 'Dad, I'm bored.'

Graham started back to the present. The sun still shone, too hot yet failing to warm his icy skin. Truffle was resting with his head on his paws.

'How can you be bored?' He put on the jovial dad act again. 'When I was your age, we'd play outside from dawn until dusk.'

'Only because you had nothing else to do in the old days.' Tim rolled his eyes.

'The old days? I'm thirty-nine, not eighty-nine.'

'Still ancient, though.'

'You cheeky devil.' He poked his son in the ribs, making him giggle. 'Do you want to head home, mate?'

'No, not yet. I just want something to *do*. Have you got your phone?'

'There's no reception.' Graham took out his smart phone and tapped the screen awake. One small bar of signal flickered in and out.

'I don't need a signal to play a game! You must have games on there.'

'Tim, you are not playing electronic games on a picnic! Screens are banned.'

'I'll tell Mum!'

Graham smiled. 'Tell her. She'll agree with me on this, at least.'

'Ohhh,' Tim complained with a rising note of frustration.

'What about that tennis ball? We could play catch.'

'Oh, the ball!' Tim jumped to his feet and pulled the repulsive yellow-grey sphere out of his pocket. 'Truffle, come on! Fetch!'

Secretly Graham was relieved. He wanted to play with his boy … but he was so tired, felled by the damned headache as if it were a spear pinning his head to the ground.

'Don't throw the ball too far,' he called as boy and dog vanished down the side of the mount. 'Don't go back into the woods. Stay where I can see you. An hour, then we'll head home, all right? Told your mum I'd have you back by six.'

They were gone. He gave in with a rueful grin and lay back, shielding his eyes from the sun with his forearm. Dreaming of Lucy. Her blue eyes and sweet, tender face. *'She doesn't look old enough to be a doctor!'* everyone said.

How her patients loved her. And so did he. He would wash the mud off Tim's trainers and brush Truffle's coat. Arrive smiling, clean and bright-eyed, with a box of her favourite chocolates.

When Lucy had dropped her guard and smiled, he'd seen tenderness in her eyes. Sadness and yearning. She was softening towards him, he was certain.

Mistakes had been made, lessons learned. There was no need to let one lapse ruin the rest of their lives. Steve the 'boyfriend' would vanish, like the invisible man when his bandages were unwound … Because it had to be Graham and Lucy again. Had to be. They both knew.

Migraines always made him fall asleep. The body needed rest and would not be denied.

Graham felt the lead tablet under his fingers. He imagined he could read the words like Braille. He pictured the inside of the temple, stuffed full of similar objects, leaf upon leaf, tons of lead pressing down. All those prayers and curses and spells scratched on lead … What were they for? He dreamed he was underneath the temple, buried beneath a great weight of rock and soil and human *intention*. These curses were not directed at multiple targets. No, every single word was focused on a single aim: that of keeping something bound, imprisoned, confined.

He struggled in half-waking nightmares, delirious. Gasping for breath.

When he opened his eyes, it was dark.

The migraine had eased, but his mouth was dry and sticky. He had no idea where he was. He was in that strange stupor where the mind wakes but the body won't move and nothing makes sense. Then he remembered …

the last sound he'd heard was Tim calling the dog to action. And hadn't he issued a warning as they went? *Don't throw the ball too far ... Told your mum I'd have you back by six.*

'Tim?'

He felt the rug beneath him, damp now. The world was a dull grey, as if dusk had only recently fallen, aided by thick cloud. Panic rose like a storm, too big to contain or fight.

'Tim? Truffle! Tim! *Tim!*'

All at once he guessed what had happened. The dog, full of terrier instincts, must have resumed digging into the mound where he'd found the lead tablet. Perhaps there was a rabbit hole or a crack in the ground. Artefacts from the ruined temple had started worming their way to the surface. Truffle had gone exploring and got stuck.

And of course Tim had followed to rescue him.

Perhaps he'd shouted for help, but Graham – fast asleep in his horrible shivery cocoon of illness – had not heard.

Hands shaking violently, Graham fumbled the phone from his shorts pocket and pressed the standby button. The screen displayed a low battery warning. He flicked the warning away, saw that the time was seven-forty.

Jesus.

He scrambled down the side of the knoll, sweat and tears streaming down his face.

'Tim, I'm not angry,' he called as he felt along the sides of the mound. Weeds tangled around his forearms. Nettles grazed his skin. 'Call out, so I know where you are.'

A whimper? His hands found a crack in the ground, like the entrance to a badger sett. Big enough to admit a terrier-sized dog, or a small boy. He tried to use the phone as a torch, but it revealed nothing and kept switching off. A black pit in the earth, that was all.

'Tim?'

He pushed his head in. A terrible stench oozed out, suffocating. A smell of wet mould, leaves rotting away to slime, dead things … The cloying sour smell of decay. He caught his breath and gagged.

'Tim! It's Dad. Say something.'

Silence.

Graham felt into the hole, deeper and deeper. He held his breath, snatching air only when he absolutely must. A couple of feet in, his fingers found something.

A fold of fabric … a sleeve?

He felt further in, plunging both hands deep. There wasn't room for his shoulders, so the action pushed his face into the side of the mound. Soil, bits of stone and twig, slimy lichen, husks, centipedes … he didn't know what lay under his hands, didn't care. He found an arm, then a small skinny torso.

His muscles and joints protested as he struggled to get a grip on the boy. Sweat ran beneath his shirt, hot and salty. His breath came fast between his clenched teeth but he endured the dreadful stench, kept his hysteria under control.

'Tim, I've got you,' He tried to sound calm and reassuring, like a rescuer. 'How did you squeeze yourself in there? It's okay, I've got you now. Can you hear me?'

No answer.

The slick of sweat on his body went cold.

'No. No no no.'

On the ground near his right hip, his phone began to ring.

Never letting go of his son, he groped for the phone with one hand and managed to hit the speakerphone icon.

He heard Lucy's voice, crackling and breaking up.

'Graham? Where the hell are you?'

An incoherent moan of pain came from his throat. He couldn't find a single word to explain this. If their son was dead, he might as well be dead too. And then … The irreparable tragedy. The estranged father who murdered his son then killed himself to spite his ex? That's what the world would see, what Lucy would see.

Or just a tragically incompetent father. If anything, that was worse.

He should yell for help.

He tried. Nothing came out but a rasp.

'Graham?' She was nearly screaming now. 'What the hell is happening? I'm here in the car park. I'm right by your car!'

While she shouted, he went on tugging, pulling at the arm with both hands. He felt the boy's body shift slightly – enough for him to get a firmer grip on the shoulders. He felt around, located the top of the head … Tim was on his front, lying face down. Seemed like he'd got so far in, then managed to turn around before the burrow had partly collapsed on him.

Carefully Graham eased the head to one side, praying that he hadn't already suffocated. At last he managed to hook his hands under both of his son's armpits.

Tim was slippery with wet soil, rotten vegetation and animal faeces, caked in it. Graham began to pull. He shook and strained with the effort. Half an inch at a time … Christ, this was like …

Flashback to Tim's birth. The obstetrician with forceps, trying to ease his son into the world while Lucy groaned and Graham stood helpless …

Then he felt a movement under the collarbone. The ribcage rose and fell with the tiniest breath. Graham cried out with relief. As he dragged his son towards the open air, a grunt of effort broke from him.

'Come on,' he said. 'Please, Tim. Please.'

'Graham!' came the furious voice again. 'Can you hear me? Now my bloody torch has gone out. I get here and find your car, and Truffle running around loose, and Tim by the car crying, but absolutely no sign of *you* …'

'Lucy, I've …'

Her voice faded and came back, yelling now. 'Tim says he got lost and couldn't find you! Truffle led him back to the car! Where the hell are you? What the *hell* were you thinking, letting them run off like that?'

It took moments for her words to sink in.

Tim, by the car …

'I've called the police. I've got to take him and Truffle home, they're exhausted, but I've called the …'

'Lucy?'

He shouted, but no answer came. She was gone. The night was huge and empty around him. Nothing came from the phone but a faint hiss of white noise, a lost connection.

The creature came out of the mound in a slithering rush and landed heavily on him as he fell backwards. It settled on his chest, snuffling the air. He saw its eyes: dim green moons set along the top of its head. Too many eyes.

Lucy returned from the hospital, tired out as always. She threw off her coat, saw the babysitter out, then pulled her son onto her knee. She hugged him close. Truffle laid his head on her thigh and gazed up at them both. The house was otherwise empty. Steve was long gone.

'No, Daddy can't come home today,' she said in response to Tim's questions.

Impossible to stay angry with a man who no longer spoke, or even blinked.

'He *does* want to see us, but he's too ill.' She stroked her son's hair. 'Yes, sweetheart, I know. I miss him too.'

FREDA WARRINGTON is the award-winning author of 21 (so far) novels of epic fantasy, sword n' sorcery, gothic vampire romance, contemporary fantasy, the supernatural and alternative history. Her work includes *A Taste of Blood Wine, Dracula the Undead, A Blackbird in Silver, The Amber Citadel, Dark Cathedral* and *Elfland*.

Dracula the Undead won the Dracula Society's Best Gothic Novel award in 1997.

Elfland won the Romantic Times Best Fantasy Novel in 2009

Her long-standing fascination with King Richard III led her to write *The Court of the Midnight King – A Dream of Richard III*, an alternative history novel about Richard with a fantasy twist. She also writes short stories, the most recent being *Ruins and Bright Towers* for the anthology *Night's Nieces* (Immanion Press, edited by Storm Constantine), a collection of tales in tribute to the late and much-missed writer Tanith Lee.

Freda lives in rural Leicestershire with her husband Mike and her widowed mother. When not writing, she enjoys reading, art, travelling, SF conventions, all things Gothic.

Visit www.fredawarrington.com.

MADSWITCH

Justina L A Robson

My mother tried to kill me again this morning. She laid in wait for me behind the kitchen door with the iron raised. In a departure from her usual MO it was plugged in. The puff of steam from the jet holes was a bit of a giveaway as I trudged down the hall in slippers and dressing gown, tea-tray held at the ready. She always used to be ironing first thing when we were little. School shirts, then trousers, after pressing Dad's shirt to perfection.

Now she forgets what she's doing halfway through getting it out and stands there, usually without even the board, iron raised in her hand. She looks quizzical, like someone pondering where they left their keys. This morning she was pressing the steam jet. I held up the tray as I walked in and the iron clonked it with a sudden jab, partly alarm – she was always defocused – and partly a desire to do harm. Her malice was crafty and casual these days. My brother called her Gollumina, because like Gollum she had two sides now, one nice and pathetically sweet because she knew we were looking after her, one filled with a primal rage that had lain a long time in hidden caves where Dad had buried it under a landslide of fists. These had been newly opened by dementia and an ancient reptilian malevolence had emerged, triggered by sudden movements or any unexpected incident, such as someone walking into a room when she was standing behind the door.

'You're losing your touch,' I said, putting the tray down and removing the iron from her very carefully before switching it off at the wall and putting it to cool in the pantry.

She pouts, her fun spoiled. 'Where's your Dad?'

Dead these twenty years. 'He died, Mum.' And not a day too soon.

'Oh. Where's the dog?'

'In the hall.'

'You have to feed him last or he'll think he's king of the house.'

'Yes, Mum.' I get her sat down and give her breakfast, and put Mark's breakfast on the table just as he comes in and sits down, eats in silence. My brother waits until Mark has gone to work. Wisely.

Mark doesn't like Andy, because Andy has nothing wrong with him but still doesn't have a job or do anything worth a tinker's damn. I am not much better. I look after Mum and the house. But at least this is not working in my old position at Nutech as lead scientist, which would have ended our relationship by now. There can only be one breadwinner to take the lead position and that should be the person who isn't the head of the household too. Man gets the job and woman gets the house. It's the way of things. Because it just is. It is here, in Todmorden, and it always has been. Why fight nature?

Anyway, I have Mum, Andy and Mark and Raffles. No job. No position. No prestige. Most importantly, even after Andy's allowances, Mum's pension and my savings, no money. Hence I have tactically kept Mark in spite of the fact that his resentment at having to part with money he has earned in order to pay his (and some of our) way is often enough to get him drunk at weekends and then the punches can fly.

I know what you're thinking. No really.

I used to think it too. I think it over and over every day once Mark has gone and Andy is safely occupied with his computer games and Mum has gone to the daycare centre for the morning. Then, after a hasty bit of cleanup and the emptying of the commode, I rush to the shed.

The shed is an old hut, some relic from WWII that my grandfather built with the notion there may be a need for something halfway between a bomb shelter and a refuge from grandma's wrath. The latter was always more of a threat in this valley. It's his workbench that holds my equipment, sheltered from mice and spiders by a large opaque Perspex box under a tarp. It's behind the gardening things. Opposite stands a woodworking bench and an old easel and some paints from two abandoned notions of artistic retreat.

Surely it would have been better to put Mum into care or stay in my job and pay for someone to look after her in the daytime? Andy can't be relied on. He has autism. Between them they could burn the house down by eleven in the morning should they get into a fatal clash of viewpoints so they must be managed separately. I can't leave Andy alone too long, just in case. Before she started to succumb to Alzheimer's Mum looked after him all the time. They are the 'dead ducks' in Mark's view. It's one of the few occasions he enjoys wheeling out his version of the survival of the fittest when the subject gets around to the fact that my days with them are no better than his days pushing insurance. Mark is not suited to a desk job. He should be in the army instead, or a football team. Somewhere that it's OK to express yourself through physical violence.

In his oft-stated post-pub view Mum and Andy should be left out for the wolves. There are no wolves in Todmorden however. The best one could do is leave them on the kerb on bin collection day and hope the Council took them away. Don't think I haven't imagined it once or twice. Maybe I'll stand there instead.

Under the Perspex box are the beautiful canisters, dishes and containers of my laboratory with their scientific corporate logos stamped in clear, precise shapes. Beside them in a sealed crate are my books and papers and my iPad plugged into the ancient sockets on the extension cord. As I get out what I need I'm reminded of Sunday School, watching the vicar remove his sacred bits and pieces from the mouldy smelling damp of the vestry and laying them on the altar. I was never sure if they had real power or not. I felt always worried about them: in case they did and they were being disrespectfully kept in a poor place and in case they didn't and we were all wasting our time on a few knickknacks.

Centrifuge, beakers, tubes, petridishes, oh you beautiful objects of light. Let us see what you have grown today. A beard of mould it seems. That's disappointing. My cultures have died and been taken over by more robust contaminants from the shed itself. Must try to avoid seeing this as a significant metaphor for my life.

I clean them out and try not to feel despondent. Science is a marathon, not a sprint. Failures are information. And this has told me that I need better hygiene during my culture preparations. Anyway, it results in me spending the first minutes of my precious time back at the sink washing up. I doubt there's anything viable in the culture gel that can't be washed down a regular drain.

Surely a woman of my intelligence shouldn't be putting up with a Neanderthal like Mark? Actually no woman, nor anyone else in a civilised society should have to put up with Mark. But thousands of people do. Love is the reason most often cited. 'Oh but I love him.' Or her. Well, I love things too, but if I'm honest, he's not one of them. Love is a kind and sweet emotion, the sort of thing you direct at kittens and children. Mark is more of a habit, like smoking, or an old piece of clothing you can't bring yourself to throw away because you wore it in happier, better times and once it looked good on you even though now it makes you look like something even people in Halifax would throw out.

My father used to work in this shed. Mum resented every second. The shed belonged to Granddad and my father's brewing projects were unwelcome tenants in its hallowed ground. She's happier now that I have it. Her paints have gone solid in their tubes but clearly I couldn't throw them out because they're hers. The brewery equipment I have laundered and put to a new use. Some of it had to be carefully replaced by glass equipment because of the chemicals and processes it now houses. I check this. Well, I might not be good at culturing germline precision-engineered bacteria yet, but I am good at manufacturing Ecstasy it seems. My MDMA, as granddad might put it, is turning out 'right nice'. It's at a stage I can leave it and I don't have time to progress it now so after admiring it and recalculating the final likely output I cover it all up again with mousy sacking.

Inside my newsgroups some people have answered my questions about E Coli re-engineering with a view to creating precursors to serotonin. They have also responded to my general call for information about oxytocin production. I read them avidly, in the way that I used to read the back of cornflakes' packets and the advertisements in women's magazines offering the latest suggestions for a happier life through the ingestion of different foods and supplements. Oxytocin binds us harmoniously together and reduces inflammation, literal and emotional. Serotonin, at the right levels, gives a sense of wellbeing and, notoriously, when it is lacking causes low mood, irritation and depression. I am far from the first person to consider engineering the large and unhappy family cell with chemistry. The MDMA is just my backup plan. I have two real plans.

The first is to use gut bacteria to treat Mom's dementia, with oxytocin boosting, thus lessening her aggression and anxiety. It won't bring back her memories or halt the progression of the deterioration but at least we might be able to traverse the house without being prey to a homicidal relative. The first plan is also useful because Andy's autism, again not curable exactly, is partly exacerbated by low blood oxytocin. If I could up that, he would feel better and be more receptive to ordinary social contact. I could also treat the apparently 'normal' Mark, since he has a low response to the ordinary methods of inducing heavy oxytocin production by natural means: cuddling and sex. He doesn't do the former (a significant sign) and he is selfishly functional at the latter, performances of note staged mostly for himself and his own sense of prowess rather than any mutual connectivity. If I want the latter I have to work hard in my imagination, rewriting the flimsy material provided into hard evidence of love and enduring affection. It's like a constant rewiring job on reality. Hard, arduous and not very rewarding. I don't so much bother since I thought of my plan and concede a point to reality by getting my own meagre fix from romance novels. I always did wonder why they were so popular among women in caring situations, as I used to go about despising them and their tawdry covers. Well, pride tossed aside, now I know. Needs must when the devil drives.

However, there is a large flaw in The Plan's original beauty of concept. Oxytocin cannot survive the environment of the gut and even if it did, both it and serotonin have a very low chance of crossing successfully into the bloodstream from there. Only their precursor chemicals are capable of that. Eat tons of turkey! Precursors aplenty in there. Our freezer is stuffed full of turkey nuggets. However, they've not been significant as far as I can see. Plus my mother doesn't like turkey and will only nibble the coating off. I was also unclear as to exactly how much turkey would be enough and what else was required. Lots of vitamin C for one thing. So I attempted to administer fruits, juices and tablets. Mark does not eat fruit. Andy does not like orange, the colour *or* the flavour. But at least Andy understands and likes the idea that there is a simple chemical formulation somewhere that would be useful to him. Mark thinks nature intended everything to be as it is and is best left alone. He cites God here as a precedent. But really he just can't be bothered to think about anything. I would say that turkey, oranges and hugs are all present in nature, but that would require we actually have the conversation in the first place. Since the last one of those ended up with him throwing me down the stairs I think the time is better spent my way.

A sound of feet on the garden gravel path makes me slam the iPad shut. Mark cannot find out about this. I race to cover it all up. Then I remember he's at work. I dash out and forestall my mother tipping herself over into the pond as she looks at the sullen face of the one goldfish that the herons have not eaten this summer.

'Fish and chips!' she says, pointing at it. Raffles stands next to her in his own doggy world, wagging his tail and looking pleased with how things have gone. 'Your Dad likes that. Where is he? This grass needs a cut. What will the neighbours think?'

'They're fine about it,' I say, glancing at the nail-scissors finish on the Marstons' lawn, their oddly flamboyant cement Victorian Lady standing in eternal *qu'elle surprise* atop their ornamental rockery. Surprise! You're in Todmorden. No wonder you look so surprised!

Then I remember she's back early from daycare. Why? An ominous feeling ticks through my bones as I ask her.

'Oh Mary brought me back,' she says with great confidence. 'We walked it. Not far is it? Just off the main street with that nice cafe thing and all their fancy hoohaa herbs, then another couple of turns, a wander and a shuffle and here we are!'

Mary was Mum's best friend when they were girls. She is still alive, in Liversedge, in an old folks' home. The Mary Mum is referring to now is strictly imaginary, and still only nine years old. I hope that when I get senile I remember my friends this way. On the other hand, this means Mum has walked out of the Centre and all the way back alone, through twenty first century traffic, equipped only with her 1940s mind. But she's here. My anger and fear and longing and strange frustration that such an adventure didn't provide me an easy way out must all die in the face of simple facts. I look at the fish. I don't know if he is Bert, Ernie, Scooter or Animal. He's one of them. The only Muppet left.

Raffles barks at him and lolls his tongue out of his mouth. If I could just make Mum into a dog … they seem to have such simple requirements. I pat Raffles and rub behind his ears and he growls and groans in total delight. Easy. Want oxytocin? Get a dog.

'Why don't you give Raffles a brush?' I suggest, going to the shed to fetch the Furminator, a fierce looking device with metal teeth like shark jaws that is perfect for long haired retrievers.

We spend half an hour grooming the dog. I get out enough hair to stuff a cushion and Mum seems pleased that effort has been made, time not wasted. I sit her outside with tea, wrapped against the English summer, and haul out our mower and do the rounds with it, hoping to buy myself a quiet evening. On the way round I consider my second plan. This is a stupid, frivolous and entirely pointless thing which gives me more delight than anything else. I am going to turn Raffles green.

There is no reason for this other than a vision I have of the early Todmorden winter, dark by five in the afternoon as I take Raffles for his evening walk. We go out of town and into the countryside where it is too black for anyone else to go, the way lit only by his glowing green coat. Dog beacon.

I'm not sure if it's cruel to dogs to make them glow green at night. But people have done worse and I wouldn't harm him. I think it's a silly thing to do, but the fact that nothing hangs on it, that it is purely an experiment for its own foolish sake, is what endears it to me. It's not as if Raffles will be having his own family or attempting to live in the wild like an urban wolf where such a thing might matter to his survival. Green dogs would probably get extra treats.

The issue of changing the hair development would mean re-engineering his melanocytes to produce one of several potential colourations instead of their present distribution of melatonin in the familiar golden Labrador argot. Bacteria have been engineered to fluoresce under blacklight in a variety of shades through a cut and replace technique that students can master. However, my plan does not involve bacterial genomes, but the rather more complicated Labrador ones. I am not even certain you could tweak a living dog, but might have to create one from scratch with the alteration made at the zygotic stage. It may be easier to make a leopard pattern dog by finding and employing the skin patterning gene sequences out of an actual leopard. My mind is full of green leopard pattern dogs by the time I am done with the grass.

Andy comes out to see what's what at that point and I go inside to discover he has emptied the fridge looking for cheese slices and left everything out and the door open. We have lunch at two. I'm done by three. I can't go back to the shed now, it's too late. I have to wait for Mark to get home so we can get through the evening and the night and then another morning before I can return.

But the next day, instead of working, I find myself looking at my father's photo. I keep it on my iPad and the real one is in the bank where nobody can destroy it by accident or on purpose. Today's emails bring difficult news. Even if I did manage to successfully transplant an engineered genome into E Coli and introduce a population into a human gut it seems that my notion of tripping larger levels of oxytocin production will be foiled by the fact that the final breakdown of the involved proteins is triggered only by the same damn nerve cells I am trying to compensate for in the first place. I'd be better off investing my money into ready-made oxytocin nasal sprays and relabeling them as flu inhibitors. In fact, that's the best idea I have had all year and would have saved an infinite amount of time and effort. Screw science, just buy the crap and then start work promoting terror of the flu among my family to ensure they snort the stuff up like socialites on coke. With any luck they'd form some addictive connection to the spray, in the way that you can form an addictive connection to anything that gives a rewarding jolt, and then ... and then ... Oh and then I don't know. I have a vision of us living in some soft focus world of bleary affection, blundering through life inebriated on feel good chemicals so we don't notice ... don't notice ...

And what is it we don't notice, Carol? I think to myself as I make myself look up the prices; grab that notion and make it more real, haul it closer, closer ... what must we not notice? We must not notice ... but at this point it always peters out, either my willingness or my sense that there is an answer to the question. I know there is. I know it is here. It follows me around like a silent, planet-sized emptiness, watching my every effort with hollow eyes. It longs for me to put it out of its misery and silence. I see it from the corner of my eye. When I am crying I always see it there, on the edge, behind me, over my shoulder, everywhere that I am not exactly looking at in any particular moment.

I look up the prices. Then I bring up my Dad's photo and I look at that. Around me the halfway done remains of my precursor generating bacterial factories sit silent, all the activity still going on virulently microscopic and utterly invisible to me, watched over by the Unnoticed Creature. It has no hope, no interest. It merely observes.

My father's buried in the worst gaveyard I have ever

been in. I'd pay everything I have never to go there again. The place fills me with a dread I cannot express and it is the place I first noticed the Creature.

The church is in his home village, which is not here, but a way away. It is inexplicably sited in a low hollow only a few feet above the height of both the river and the canal, nearly hidden in a clutch of woodland down a cobbled lane. The yard lies across the running water, as if the church jumped onto an islet in fear, having remembered that ancient protection against the undead. It has an empty, abandoned feeling in spite of the fresh flowers, the gardened edges, the tidied path. Like the mills that paid for it it feels like it is one more mill, the final one, through which to process families in their final rendering – it's impersonal, too stoney, too big, devoid of anything but the power to host the Creature when it retreats there to brood and ponder.

Superficially the graveyard is pretty, maintained – I suppose because there are an odd number of children's graves there, it seems to me. Babies, with mouldering toys and blankets tied to their fresh headstones. Children, plot covered in action figures going through a final inexplicable war, in Barbies trying to be cheerful and fashionable and pink under the rotting lilacs. Plastic that won't rot, only pale in the sun. Many graves are fenced in with gilded, low palisades which only serve to make them look more pathetically vulnerable. The things you love we bring you here, I thought once there, on that day. We leave you here. Down in the dark with the water and the Creature. How could anybody leave you here? How do we?

I talk to Dad. I don't believe he is in that yard of course. I don't believe he is in his image. He has gone and we are alone. I look at him, a bit like me, stubborn seeming to be the trait we have most in common, that and pragmatism and a kind of Yorkshire expectation of if not the worst, then not the best. Mustn't grumble. They don't have enough to eat in Africa. It's just a bit o' rain.

I must view these things only as setbacks. Just a bit o' rain. Serotonin precursors look more hopeful. I could still conceivably create bacteria who will produce L-Tryptophan.

The Creature looks at me sadly. *What about Serotonin Syndrome?* It says, lugubriously expanding to fill every unfilled piece of space in the universe. *Even if you create a flood of serotonin there will come a reckoning. Body uses up things, gets low on supplies, then mood falls, inevitable, you don't know the dose, you don't know the threshold, you just don't know, Carol.* **You don't know.**

Monkey, Dad says, smiling, ruffling my hair. He can't see The Creature any more. It doesn't matter to him. He never saw it, even though it is what drove him and drives Mark when they switch over from kindness into hate. *You little Monkey.*

Monkey is sad. Monkey likes green dogs. Monkey does not like the Creature. Why does the Creature stare? What does it want? Under the bed and out from under. Takes things and ponders them in its big, ugly fingers. Mum's memory. Andy's ability to feel things like others do. Mark's kindness. Dad. What's it doing with them all?

Don't cry, Carol. Think about Tryptophan. Crying is pointless but Tryptophan exists and is real and it could be helpful, even if only a little bit. But don't cry, Carol. Someone has to keep it together here and it looks like that is going to be you.

It's funny that I have to talk to myself in the third person because nobody else is here.

The Creature has a point about Serotonin Syndrome

sadly. I see that now. I have a feeling that the MDMA and oxytocin dreams will fall on the same hurdle. The problem is that everything is a finite resource and the body is a finely tuned system for dealing with that. Tolerance rises and sensitivity falls. More stimulants are required to produce the effect. Eventually there cannot be enough stimulant and the effect catastrophically fails. Falling, we are plunged into the abyss.

I don't think I can fix it and I don't know what I will do if I can't.

Don't cry, Carol. Crying doesn't help. We have to get on with things. Can't sit here all day feeling sorry for yourself.

But I'm out of ideas. I ask the Creature, purely because it's there and won't leave me alone. It can't, I think. Now I've seen it once, it can't pretend it doesn't exist any more. Even looking at it makes my whole body shake in mortal dread. Of course I know it. Everyone knows it. And it knows them. We can't hide from each other.

'My name today,' says the Creature, 'is T GONDII.'

Unusual for it to speak like that, in an actual address and not simply by presence alone. The name does ring a bell. Toxoplasmosis, a parasitical infection primarily passed by cats, but infesting many or most human adults, in its active form is known to occupy many parts of the human body. In its active form it produces high levels of dopamine such that it is suspected to play a significant role in schizophrenia and other neurotransmitting malfunction situations.

I could plausibly re-engineer the genome of *T Gondii* to create oxytocin instead. Then if it goes too far, yes, it will run into the MDMA issue: too much Ecstasy, in copying oxytocin on the receptors, uses up too much transmission fluid and ends up leaving you on a worse low. In bacteria, even those functioning with a madswitch that toggles their activity on and off in response to the surroundings, I could easily get the proportions completely wrong. Overbreeding could be catastrophic. Eat a Mars bar, chill out, and a day later jump into the canal to end it all. Tempting in some respects... But *T Gondii*, whatever else it does, exists only at minor influence levels and excretes in such a way that it clearly leaves most people perfectly functional, if somewhat over-attracted to cats. If I change that output to oxytocin it will leave them in a better mood, cat or no cat.

With the emergence of a plan the Creature shrinks. I know it is an illusion that human beings are a problem that is amenable to the fixings of logic and science. The Creature itself will not be banished. Every day he finds another name. But he can be warded off here and there. Although I fear to push hard. He has a way of creeping back through the cracks. Tomorrow his name will be Malaria. Tomorrow he will mutate into another form and burrow deeper and become entrenched in an unassailable compound.

But today I just have time to read some papers and make some orders. It will be a budget blower.

It takes more than eighteen months even with the help of every resource I can muster to transform the local cat *T Gondii* into *T Carolii*. I spend another six months practising and fine tuning until they are robust and viable. I know it's not ethical really, but I test them on next door's cat. It has spent its adult life leaving richly disgusting piles of crap on our grass that must be picked, bagged and disposed of, so I find it hard to feel bad. Flushing cat soil down the toilet leads to massive T

Gondii infection in the general population, where treatment isn't capable of accounting for it all. Useful to know. Meanwhile Tinkerbell the calico longhair has a taste for tinned salmon I'm only too happy to exploit. I'm not sure what oxytocin does to cats.

Tinkerbell has grown fatter and more docile, shows less inclination to hunt and more to lying in the sun under the greenhouse glass. However, since I wasn't a great observer of her before it's hard to say if this is due to the T Carolii or some other situation. But, analysis of Tinkerbell's deposits reveals a constant presence of T Carolii cysts in addition to much fewer T Gondii. So my population, whatever else it does, lives on in one fat and idle cat.

I am not sure whether I should go ahead and infect the family without asking them. I feel sure that if my parasite works as intended it could have far reaching beneficial uses for humanity. Oxytocin has done well in ameliorating the worst of dementia and autism, increasing contentment and promoting wellbeing. It helps those in despair deal with their version of the Creature and what torment it brings.

However, it does strike me that administering it falsely, as it were, my sneaking it in as a chemical or by my methods is a kind of counterfeit love. All the benefits of love or at least of warm contact and good intent, and none of the real affection. Even if I was administering it with that intent it's not my hands that touch, not my voice that speaks the words of acceptance. I am wracked by doubt now, ethical and scientific both. But like much human action I also think that my rationalisation is too late and purely academic. In giving T Carolii to

Tinkerbell, I have already released it into the world in an uncontrollable way without ever having understood the greater function and community within which the original T Gondii operated and without consulting a single other being who may be affected by its survival, spread or dominion.

I would like to be saved from all I have done, and undone. But these, like my father and his inexplicable motivation to be so kind and also so cruel at the same time, stretch ever further away in time, untouchable. I seen them clearly only in hindsight, amazed at my overweening arrogance, and regrets or not they can't be changed. The Creature nods at me from her everywhere bed. *You have it right, Carol, she says. So, what now, love? What will it be? Onward in folly or stand and pretend the precipice is before us when it is behind?* And I say to her, 'It's not so much folly as what you can do, why … that's the thing you eat in the hours of the morning, three and five, awake in the dark with only yourself to abide it.'

The Creature hovers in the background expectantly. It enjoys the knowledge that in my efforts not to move or decide I have moved, and decided. When I read back over my journal entries I realise I have taken too much upon myself. But nonetheless, it is done.

I won't do it yet. I will leave it and work on the greening of the dogs. I don't want to work with skin grafts but I think I could reasonably administer the cellular treatment as a grooming spray.

My mother tried to kill me again today but in a more halfhearted way than usual. She didn't bother to hold up the iron at all, instead she attempted to make porridge and set a teatowel on fire by lighting the wrong burner and leaning too close with it wrapped around the pot handle. The alarm went off like a screeching metal rooster and Andy came down screeching in counterpoint to it, hands over his ears, barefoot and wild with terrors. He set Mum off into a secondary howling of her own, bewilderbeasted, as I struggled to flick the towel off the grip and into the sink using the wooden porridge spoon. Finally it went out on its own, in spite of me, and I was able to get up on the stool and use the spoon end to prod the alarm button.

Andy continued to yodel, having discovered he rather liked the resonance of what he was doing and the impressive noise level, finding it comforting because he could listen to it for its own sake, removed from any sense of things being wrong. Mum wittered at the table crossly, knowing it was her fault and trying to explain that the pots should have handles, not be cast iron monstrosities and can't we have something modern for once, those nonstickers with the wood.

Mark appeared, shock-headed, staring at us all, his expression outraged and comically perplexed at the same time. While he was fishing around for words I got down from the stool and said, 'It's all right. Just a false alarm. Go get dressed and I'll make your sandwiches.'

I watched his face, that struggle between being bothered to work up to self-righteousness and another, more recent temptation – not to bother with it, to turn and leave it alone, to do as he's told for the sake of getting back to the peaceful state that was broken, even if the cost is something to him. He looked at me and I went over, against all my natural inclination really, and hugged him. Confusion made him blink.

'Yer all mad,' he said, but quietly. He hugged me back briefly as if not realising what he was doing.

'Definitely,' I said with a smile, making light of what can't be got rid of.

Andy was too loud to say more but he stopped when his breakfast was put down in the right spot at the right time. By then Mark was back and Mum was eating her porridge and for a few minutes of silence you'd never know there was a thing wrong with any of us.

I took my medicine. I thought maybe it wasn't them. Maybe it was me. And since then I've slowly begun to feel better.

I opened a tin of dog food and forked it out into Raffles' bowl. He came tick a tick across the kitchen tiles and waved the plume of his emerald green, leopardskin patterned tail.

'Did something happen to the dog?' Mum asked, looking at him, as if she really couldn't see it.

Andy grinned at me. 'Green dog is green! Carol made him.'

'It's just a spray from the pet store,' I said calmly. 'They're all the rage.' And so they are: you can get pink, purple, red, nearly any colour and pattern you like, for any pet. And I make ten pence a can but nobody knows about that except me.

Today when Mum has gone to daycare and Andy is on the computer I take Raffles for a walk to the graveyard. I ignore the things that used to upset me, and I don't see the Creature, only now and again, smaller and less important than it used to be. I stand by the porcelain photograph of Dad and toss down the fabric pink roses I brought with me. The sun shines on them and their plastic raindrops. From a short distance you really wouldn't know them from the real thing.

JUSTINA ROBSON was born in Yorkshire, England in 1968. After completing school she dropped out of Art College, then studied Philosophy and Linguistics at York University. She sold her first novel in 1999 which also won the 2000 amazon.co.uk Writers' Bursary Award.

She has been a student (1992) and a teacher (2002, 2006) at The Arvon Foundation, in the UK, (a centre for the development and promotion of all kinds of creative writing). She was a student at Clarion West, the US bootcamp for SF and Fantasy writers, in 1996.

Her eleven books have been variously shortlisted for most of the major genre awards, including her latest novel *Glorious Angels*. An anthology of her short fiction, *Heliotrope*, was published in 2012. In 2004 Justina was a judge for the Arthur C Clarke Award on behalf of The Science Fiction Foundation.

Her novels and stories range widely over SF and Fantasy, often in combination and often featuring AIs and machines who aren't exactly what they seem.

She is the proud author of *The Covenant of Primus* (2013) – the Hasbro-authorised history and 'bible' of *The Transformers*.

She lives in t'North of England with her partner, three children, a cat and a dog.

DON'T BITE YOUR NAILS

David J Howe

'Don't bite your nails!'

This was the mantra that I got from my parents throughout my childhood. Quite why I shouldn't do this, I wasn't sure. There were never any penalties mentioned … but biting your nails was a no-no.

Of course I was a good boy, and so I tried very hard not to bite them. When I was younger, and the temptation to nibble became too much, my parents obtained a substance called 'Stop 'n' Grow' or some such from the chemist, and painted it onto my nails in much the same way as mum might put nail varnish on her own. Except that this stuff tasted horrendous. A cross between sick and sour lemons. Disgusting. That helped me remember not to let my fingers drift to my mouth and for the nibbling to begin.

Later in life, when my nails grew, I'd clip them with clippers. The only problem with this was that the pieces of nail would zing across the room like ninja shuriken, vanishing into the carpet, the walls and the furniture. I thought nothing of it, but carried on.

It was only when I got my own apartment that everything all went wrong.

It was Halloween, the night when all things spooky and creepy come out of the woodwork to cause mischief. It was also my first Halloween in a place on my own. My parents had finally allowed me to flee the nest, and with a job in a local butcher, I had enough money to pay the insane rent on a small flat in town. This suited me, as with the newfound independence came the possibility of getting a girlfriend … and inviting her back to mine. It was exciting, I can tell you.

So on this particular Halloween, I had been invited to a party, and so prepared myself as best I could. I had a bath, washed my hair, and prepared my outfit for the party. I had decided to go as Count Dracula, or at least some approximation of the Count. It was a fairly easy outfit to get together, and didn't look too strange. At least not as strange as dressing up as Frankenstein's monster or the Mummy or something.

Anyway. As part of my ablutions, I cut my nails. And as always, the pieces of nail flew all over my apartment. It didn't seem to matter how close I held my hand to the rubbish bin, the pieces still went everywhere. I didn't give them a second thought … after all, they had flown all over my parents' house and it never seemed to upset anyone.

After finishing my nails, I checked myself in the mirror and headed out. Maybe this would be the night I met that special girl!

It was late, or should that be early, when I got back home. The party had been something of a washout. Oh, sure, there were lots of girls there. Lots of hot girls too, dressed in low-cut revealing outfits of lace and velvet, pretending to be cute cats in high-cut leotards and tights, and one even was dressed as a mummy, except that the bandages were artfully positioned to reveal as much breast and thigh as she could without being arrested! But all the girls had boyfriends, or were with gaggles of their own pals, and a solitary, fairly shy vampire wasn't going to get a look in.

Ah well. I enjoyed sitting at the side window shopping and dreaming about what might have been. At least the beer was cold.

When I got back to my apartment, it was freezing. The winter was setting in, and I hadn't quite figured out how the heating worked as yet. So as I opened the door, it was as though a chill wave washed over me.

I reached for the light switch and snapped it on. The hallway was illuminated for a second before it went dark again. The light had been switched off again.

I frowned and blinked in the darkness. I had caught a flash of my hallway in the light before it was extinguished, and something had been wrong.

The front door shut behind me, trapping me in the darkness, and I reached out to turn on the light again. As my hand grew closer to the switch, it brushed against something soft and warm. Skin. I pulled back quickly, not quite knowing what to make of it.

Then I moved my hand again, slowly, towards the light switch and turned it on.

The light filled the hall, and my eyes looked in astonishment at what I saw.

Growing and emerging from the walls and floor were hands ... I shook my head. This couldn't be happening. It wasn't possible. But as I looked, I saw the hands and fingers moving gently, sensing the air as though they were some sort of strange underwater seaweed.

There was a hand close to the light switch, and this

was what I had brushed against. As I watched, it swayed and then moved towards the switch. With a swift motion, the fingers pushed against the switch and the hallway was plunged into darkness again. Silent except for the gentle movement of fingers in the air.

I wasn't sure what to do. I wasn't even sure that this was real. Maybe someone had slipped something into my drink at the party and this was some insane drug-induced trip.

I shuffled on my feet. Maybe if I turned the light on again, I could get to the kitchen before it went off again. I decided that this might be the best thing to do. At least there I could use the house phone – I couldn't afford a mobile as yet – and get some help.

I reached out again and turned the light on, then, taking care to avoid all the hands growing from the carpet, I stepped quickly along the corridor and into the kitchen, switching the kitchen light on even as the hall light went off again.

The kitchen was at least not as infested with the limbs as the hallway had been, but they were still there, projecting from the counter, and one was emerging from the side of the cooker, almost as though someone was stuck down beside it. I peered down there carefully, looking to see if it was in fact one of my friends playing a Halloween prank on me. But no. The hand joined a small stump of arm which was somehow fused to and growing from the floor.

I had no idea what to do. I absently reached for a glass to get myself some water, but there was a hand and arm emerging from the sink. It waved at me and the fingers somehow made contact with my own arm ... it was warm and soft, like a baby's hand. I pulled away and the glass flew from my hand, smashing on the floor and sending fragments of glass all over the place.

I swore. That was all I needed. Broken glass everywhere to have to clean up. I don't think it had quite registered with me what I was going to do with all the hands at this point.

One of the hands crawled its way blindly across the floor, moving like some great tarantula that was attached to an arm. It came to some of the glass, and after testing it gently, picked it up. It then quickly dropped it, and I saw that red blood was marking the fingers. It had cut itself. And what's more, it had known it had cut itself, and had reacted as though it hurt.

My head started to hurt. Not only was my apartment full of hands, and the floor covered with glass ... but I had no idea how to cope with any of it. I wasn't even sure I had a dustpan and brush anywhere ...

When you move into a new place, it takes time to collect all the accoutrements of independence ... they don't just appear by magic. And some you don't get until you need them ...

I remembered that I had a torch in the cupboard at least, and so got that. To my amazement it worked! Usually torches left for emergencies in cupboards have either batteries or bulbs that don't work, and often both! But this lit up just fine.

I headed out into the hallway again letting the torch guide me through the maze of hands. I noticed them drift towards the light as though they were attracted to it, but when they got close, they shied away as though it hurt them somehow.

In my bedroom, the plague of hands was worse. They were growing from my bed, the walls, the floor ... everywhere I looked I saw hands waving in the air.

One brushed my leg and gently held my ankle ... I

pulled away, feeling the hand tense as I did so, reluctant to release its grip.

As I stood there playing the light over the room, I felt completely lost. I had no idea what was happening, or what I was supposed to do. That was when the doorbell rang.

Immediately panic set in. What was I supposed to do now? Maybe they would go away. Maybe they were trick or treaters … But then I remembered that it was something like one in the morning. No-one should be up and going from door to door this late.

The doorbell rang again.

I headed into the hall, keeping clear of the hands as I went. I poked my head out and looked at the front door. The letterflap opened and a voice called, 'Are you there dear? It's your Mum!'

Mum! What was she doing here?

'Open the door, dear,' she called. 'We just need a chat.'

Reflex kicked in, and I stumbled down the darkened corridor to the front door. I pulled it open, and there indeed was my Mum and Dad.

Dad was carrying a roll of black bin liners, and a canvas sack, and Mum was smiling at me kindly.

'Hello, dear,' she said, as if it was perfectly normal for her to be on my doorstep in the middle of the night. She looked past me into the hallway.

'Oh dear. Look Thomas. We seem to be just in time.'

Dad – Thomas – peered into my apartment and nodded. 'Just in time,' he echoed.

Mum and Dad bustled into the hallway and ushered me back into the kitchen.

'Now don't worry, son. This won't take long,' said Dad.

'What won't take long?' I managed to ask, but Mum just smiled at me.

'Been cutting your nails have you?' she asked, gesturing around the kitchen.

'What? Um. Yes,' I said, raising my hand so that she could see that my nails were neatly clipped.

'I know,' she said. 'Shame we never got the chance to explain to you … but the opportunity never came.'

'Explain to me,' I said. 'Explain what? What's happening?'

Dad appeared at the door. He was holding one of the black sacks, but it was now full of something. And the something was moving.

'Soon have this lot cleared up,' he said, and vanished back out into the hall.

I could hear a gently swishing sound, and frowned as I tried to work out what was happening.

'That will do nicely,' said Mum, and I turned to see that she had removed one of the carving knives from the kitchen drawer.

She smiled, and proceeded to grab one of the hands. It gripped her own hand, and with the other she sliced at it with the knife. There was that swishing sound, and the hand and arm was sliced free of the counter. It was bleeding and dripping red onto the surface, but Mum deftly turned and threw it into one of the bin liners. Then she reached down and did the same with the one growing from under the cooker.

I felt sick. My Mum and Dad were cutting the things off and placing them in the bags. I watched as she worked, methodically harvesting all the hands and arms. As she cut each off, the stump that was left behind started to blacken and rot. It was amazing how fast it happened. There was that gentle swishing sound and the flesh, or whatever it was, sizzled and started to dissolve.

Dad dumped another two bags into the kitchen. 'Soon be done,' he said with a grin.

I watched as he and Mum worked their way around my flat, cutting off all the limbs and placing them in the bags. I wondered what on earth was going on. How could this be normal.

There was a clattering sound beside me, and I looked down to see that one of the hands, emerging from the side of the fridge, had got into the cutlery drawer, and was holding a knife in its own hand. Whether to defend itself or some other reflex action I didn't know, but as I pulled back in surprise, it lunged at me.

The knife caught my own hand, and I winced as sharp pain shot through me and a gentle swishing sound reached my ears. Mum was there immediately. She grabbed the knife from the hand and with a swift motion of her own knife, sliced it free.

'Let me have a look at that,' she said.

I let her look at my own hand. The knife had sliced across my fingers, and they burned. I saw that, in fact, one of my fingers had been severed. It was there on the floor.

I went light headed. Not quite believing what I was looking at. More horrific was my hand. The end of the finger which had been severed was rapidly blackening, dissolving in the same way as the remaining stumps had.

'Oh dear,' said Mum. 'We'd hoped for longer than this with you, son.'

'What do you mean?' I asked, the light headedness spreading rapidly.

'Well,' she said. 'It's the nails you see?'

I shook my head. Not seeing at all.

'The nails! It's the same as planting seeds. You take cuttings from the young plants, transplant them to fresh soil, and then they grow and create new plants. It's the same.'

I nodded, not really understanding at all. My whole arm was burning now, and I could see my flesh dissolving as I watched.

'Thomas?' called Mum out the door. 'Keep a good one will you? We'll need it.'

'Right you are,' said Dad.

'Don't you worry,' said Mum. 'We knew this would be hard on you, but you're the first who has insisted on going it alone ... heading out into the world. We couldn't see the harm ... but then there's the whole thing with the nail clippings ... we keep an eye you see ...'

I didn't see. In fact, everything had gone black. The last thing I remembered was Mum moving the black bin liners around, making room for something ...

It was Halloween, the night when all things spooky and creepy come out of the woodwork to cause mischief. And as usual I was spending it at home with Mum and Dad. They doted on me ... raised me well ... tried to keep me on the straight and narrow ...

And made sure that I never bit my nails.

DAVID J HOWE has been involved with *Doctor Who* research and writing for over thirty years. He has been consultant to a large number of publishers and manufacturers for their *Doctor Who* lines, and is author or co-author of over thirty factual titles associated with the show. He also has one of the largest collections of *Doctor Who* merchandise in the world.

David was contributing editor to *Starburst* Magazine for seventeen years from 1984 – 2001. From 1994 he was book reviews editor for *Shivers* Magazine until it ceased publication in 2008. In addition he has written articles, interviews and reviews for a wide number of publications, including *Fear, Dreamwatch, Infinity, Stage and Television Today, The Dark Side, Doctor Who Magazine, The Guardian, Film Review, SFX, Sci-Fi Entertainment, Collectors' Gazette, Deathray, Doctor Who Insider* and the *Oxford Dictionary of National Biography*.

He edited the bi-monthly newsletter of the British Fantasy Society from 1992 to 1995, and also edited and published several books for them, including the British and World Fantasy Award shortlisted *Manitou Man*, a limited edition hardback and paperback collection of short fiction by horror author Graham Masterton. He was Chair of the BFS from 2010 to 2011, and edited their fortieth anniversary anthology, *Full Fathom Forty*, published in September 2011.

He wrote the book *Reflections: The Fantasy Art of Stephen Bradbury* for Dragon's World Publishers and has contributed short fiction to *Peeping Tom, Dark Asylum, Decalog, Dark Horizons, Kimota, Perfect Timing, Perfect Timing II, Missing Pieces, Shrouded by Darkness, Murky Depths, Terror Tales of London* and *Flesh Like*

Smoke and factual articles to *James Herbert: By Horror Haunted, The Radio Times Guide To Science Fiction* and *1001 Television Series To See Before You Die*. He wrote the screenplay for *Daemos Rising*, a film released on DVD by Reeltime Pictures in 2004, and was contributing writer for *White Witch of Devil's End*, a drama in production by Reeltime Pictures. A book of his fiction, *talespinning*, appeared from Telos Publishing in September 2011.

He is Editorial Director of Telos Publishing Ltd, a UK based independent press specialising in horror/science fiction Novellas, crime novels, and guides to a variety of film and TV shows. In 2006 the company won the World Fantasy Award for their publishing work, and in 2010 celebrated their tenth anniversary while also receiving the British Fantasy Award for Best Small Press for two consecutive years in 2010 and 2011. He currently contributes liner notes for BBC Audio's range of *Doctor Who* novelisation CDs and *Doctor Who* merchandise details for the *Doctor Who: The Complete History* partwork for Hachette/Panini.

WALKING THE DEAD

Sam Stone

Granny died in front of the telly watching her favourite soap. One minute she was keeled over, drool slipping between her false teeth, a last hiss gurgling in her throat and the next she was going about her business like nothing had happened. At first, I was the only one who noticed there was something wrong and it even took *me* a day or two to realise she was a zombie.

I was eating a Chinese take-out at the time and when I saw dear old granny slump I started yelling as loudly as I could.

'Oh my Gawd. Mum! Granny's pegged it.'

Mum came rushing in of course, but much to her disappointment Granny didn't look any worse off than before, so she clouted me round the ear.

'Fancy getting my hopes up like that, you little bugger.'

The wandering was a bit of a worry at first. If she got outside she couldn't seem to find her way back, but being at home she was, as Mum always said, 'happy as Larry'. Not that I could ever figure out who this 'Larry' was but it didn't seem to matter in the scheme of things.

A few days later I heard about a friend's uncle getting up off the morgue slab just as they were about to cut him open. Then there was the butcher down the road who got trapped in his own fridge over the weekend. When his assistant arrived at work on Monday morning he found him unconscious on the fridge floor, but within minutes he was up and about, preparing orders. It was weird that his wife hadn't claimed him missing but I think she was hoping he'd run off with one of the women he chatted up in the shop.

We were at school when old Mr Chipperton croaked it during the exam. I was picking my nose and flicking the bogies at snobby Billy 'call me William' Price.

'Sir? Sir?' shouted Billy and everyone looked up and around the room to see what was going on. 'Sir? Someone keeps flicking *things* at me!'

Mr Chipperton didn't move. Everyone knew he liked to take a nap from time to time but he usually reacted quickly when someone spoke. Gemma Smith was the first one to get up and prod him, then I went over and it was just like my old granny, all flaked out and drooly.

'He's dead,' I pointed out. 'Better go and get the Head.'

Gemma took the news in good spirit. Dead things didn't bother her, unlike everyone else. She held the record for being the 'grossest' girl in school – she even dissected a squirrel we once found. She'd flipped out her pocket knife long before the rest of us reached her. I remember it was all full of maggots and Sophie Price threw up on the pavement when she saw them wriggling around in the squirrel's stomach.

Gemma looked at Old Chipperton, pinching and pulling at him until she was satisfied I was right, then ran off to get the head mistress, Ms Havers. The rest of the kids just sat there, watching the body. I think they weren't really sure if it was a joke. I am a bit of a prankster, and I'd roped Gemma in many times to back up some tall tale or other, so it was understandable that they didn't trust us.

A few minutes later Ms Havers came in with the first aider and they had Old Chipperton on the floor giving him mouth to mouth, but clearly nothing could be done.

'Go into the hall,' said Ms Havers to the class.

She sent Gemma back to the office to tell them to call an ambulance and to send someone down to the hall to look after the kids there.

I stayed behind in the class room to act as a runner. Ms Havers was sitting with the body and, as the ambulance men entered the room, Old Chipperton suddenly stood up.

As we all looked on, mouth open with surprise, Mr Chipperton returned to his seat in front of the class and gazed around rather confused.

'Has the bell gone?' he said at which point, Ms Havers, who'd been too stunned to speak at first, began to scream her head off like she'd lost her mind.

You see, she cottoned on pretty quickly that Old Chipperton was actually still dead and not revived. I think it was something to do with the blueness around the mouth and this awful vacant expression he had. Ms Havers picked up a chair and ran at Mr Chipperton. The ambulance men were a bit shocked, but fortunately one of them reacted by taking her down in a rugby tackle. It all got a bit ugly then. Ms Havers kicked one of the men in the crunches and while he was down, heaving his guts up, she somehow managed to untangle herself from the other one. She crawled agilely across the floor and pulled herself up by holding onto Mr Chipperton's desk. Then she reached for the paperweight and attempted to smash in the old man's brains.

The ambulance men took her away and, after giving

him the once over, they left Old Chipperton behind.

'Yep,' said the paramedic. 'You're definitely dead. No heart beat or pulse and your colour is decidedly deprived of oxygen.'

'Oh,' said Mr Chipperton. 'What should I do then?'

'Go home and take two aspirins…' answered the other paramedic, now recovered from Ms Havers' well aimed kick. 'That's what we usually recommend when we don't know what else to do.'

Mr Chipperton picked up his hat and coat and headed for the exit as Ms Havers was wheeled away, suitably drugged and strapped down for her own, and Old Chipperton's, safety. At the door Mr Chipperton paused and looked around. I was still at a loss as to what to do, so I stayed at my desk watching the proceedings. I can't say I wasn't alarmed by it all. It was a bit weird. But what I'd noticed with my Granny was that she had carried on just like she hadn't died. Except she didn't eat or go to the toilet anymore, which pleased my mum because at least she wasn't wetting the bed on Saturday night after she'd had her regular bottle of stout. In fact she didn't want her stout at all now. All she wanted to do was shuffle around and watch *Coronation Street*. I always thought you had to be dead to watch that programme anyway…

Mr Chipperton on the other hand seemed to have retained full use of his speech.

'Are you alright, Sir?' I asked eventually.

'Yes, thank you. Charlie, isn't it?'

'Yes, Sir.'

'I seem to have forgotten my way home.'

'Oh don't worry. My granny does that as well. I'll take you to the office and get the address.'

I didn't mind helping Old Chipperton and I walked him home that night.

School was closed for a few days to help us kids get over the shock of what happened. Ms Havers didn't come back after that. She became one of the 'Hysterics' and as soon as they let her out of hospital she began the anti-dead group ZADPATEY which basically meant, 'Zombies Are Dead People And They Eat You'. What can I say? She is a teacher and they seem to love acronyms no matter how crap they are. But she had some success with it, got a group of followers together, and suddenly there was a campaign against zombies.

The world went to shit a bit after that. More people died, rose again and general panic ensued. When the reports of the dead reviving and then 'walking' started to filter through, the papers and the news channels, as usual, made a meal of it all: implying that zombies were going to make a meal of us. Naturally that led to mass panic.

Of course, I understood why people were scared. It's not every day a group of dead people surround you, reach out and generally groan – sometimes incoherently – that they needed help. The majority of the living were naturally afraid and ran like hell, occasionally bashing in a zombie brain or two for good measure.

'It's a natural survival instinct to run from the unknown,' said our biology teacher. 'People are just like primates when it all comes down to it. And we don't like being around dead bodies – they smell for a start.'

'But, Sir,' I said. 'I haven't noticed anything different about the way the zombies smell ... and as far as I know they haven't actually hurt anyone.'

'Not yet, Charlie my boy,' answered the teacher. 'But give them time...'

'This is crazy,' said Gemma as we hung around the school yard. 'They are talking about closing the school and Old Chipperton isn't allowed on the premises.

Personally I'd rather have a zombie sleeping at the front of the class than that dreadful supply teacher.'

'What's wrong with the supply? Other than the usual…' I asked.

'He looks like a paedo.'

'Yeah,' said Billy, who seemed to have toughened up with the thought of a coming apocalypse. 'They'll let anyone teach these days.'

'Did you see Ms Havers on the telly last night?' asked Gemma.

'She's lost it,' I said.

'If you ask me,' said Billy. 'It's racist.'

At that moment I saw a zombie hanging around outside the gates and realised it was Old Chipperton.

'Better take him home,' I said. 'Otherwise someone will mistake him for a flasher again.'

A few days later there were vans travelling up and down the streets picking up the stray zombies. They seemed to like to congregate in the middle of the road, or in malls. Okay, so it was causing an obstruction for drivers, and scaring away the shoppers, but it seemed grossly unfair to me that they were being locked up just for wandering around. It wasn't as if they were causing a riot or damaging people's property.

'What you going to do with that zombie?' I asked one of the soldiers on the rounds.

'We're just taking him away somewhere for his own protection.'

'We've all heard that before,' mumbled Mum and she took my hand – which was *really* embarrassing – and dragged me back home.

We had to hide granny for a while after that, and when she did go out I pretended she was helping *me* find my way home.

The zombie collections were all over the news and Ms Havers loved the attention of rallying the world against the defenceless dead. The crowd behind her was screaming and shouting at the cameras, but Ms Havers looked really calm and dignified. Her hair was all loose and wavy and she was actually wearing lots of make-up. I'd never seen her look like that before. It was as though she loved being on camera and was trying really hard to be a celebrity.

'Zombies are a danger to us all,' she said calmly. 'Fortunately the security services have now recognised that danger and are beginning to remove this threat from our streets.'

'Ms Havers?' shouted a man from the crowd. 'Do you know what they are *doing* to our dead relatives?'

'Well, if they've any sense they'll put a bullet clean through their dead brains and put them down permanently.'

That's when the riot broke out and the camera was jostled, the news reporter was knocked over and Ms Havers was dived on by an entire mob of unhappy families whose dead had been incarcerated.

It was only natural that a new campaign started soon after. This group was called FreeZom which was obviously a play on the words 'Freedom' and 'Zombies'. FreeZom's campaign became popular within days. No one wanted their dead shot through the brain without first proving they were dangerous. Also, people quickly realised that if nature decided their time was up, they'd rise again as well, and the first thing they'd see when they came round would be the barrel of a soldier's rifle. As if the thought of dying when you *didn't* know what would happen wasn't bad enough! So naturally FreeZom got support from many people. Even those in high places. It was rumoured that Prince Philip was giving financial support to the cause. This did give rise to some speculation that the Queen may already be among the dead and he just wasn't admitting it: but other than the usual wan expression and constantly waving hand – which was the same for all public appearances for years anyway – there really wasn't much evidence to support this view.

Walking back from school was a bit like travelling through a warzone. There were demonstrations on every street corner. One day I came across FreeZom and ZADPATEY on the opposite sides of the road. Some soldiers were trying to round up a small group of zombies who'd congregated in the middle of the street.

'I can't find my way home,' said one of the zombies. She was a small child with a blood stain down the front of her dress. She was dragging her leg, ankle all twisted the wrong way and her arm looked like it was dangling down at her side.

'I'll help you,' said one of the men from ZADPATEY to the little girl.

'Stay away from that zombie child you murdering freak!' shouted a woman from FreeZom as she ran out into the street.

The creepy guy from ZADPATEY made a grab for the poor zombie who screamed and ran, well sort of shambled really, and hid behind the army truck.

A riot broke out between the two factions as they surged across the street converging in the middle of the road.

'Bloody hell,' said a soldier. 'Not again.'

The soldiers waded in, trying to break up the fight. This was good news for the zombies they were trying to round up, of course, and they took the opportunity to

wander away from the trouble and stumble back home –
if they could find it.

I took the zombie girl's hand and led her away as fast
as her trailing leg could manage. Around the next corner
we found her bike, all crushed and bloody.

'Did someone knock you over?' I asked.

'Yep. Next door neighbour… Then, when I woke up,
he rang the soldiers to come and get me,' she said.

'Harsh.'

We found the little girl's mother beating the neighbour
around the head with a broken umbrella.

'Just wait till one of your family dies. It wasn't bad
enough that you ran my girl down; you had to turn her in
as well. You murdering bastard!'

The neighbour skulked away when the kid's mother
saw her broken child limping towards her.

'Thank you so much,' cried the mother who turned out
to be a nurse. She quickly popped her daughter's
dislocated shoulder back into place. 'Come inside and
we'll patch up that leg …'

'Best put an address label on her from now on,' I
suggested.

I watched them go in doors. It gave me a strangely
peculiar feeling of satisfaction that I'd helped them. I
turned around and went home, hoping that one day
someone would do the same for me.

That night *Corrie* was interrupted by a news flash.
Granny got mega irritated and started pacing the room as
her routine was completely disrupted.

*'Investigators into the recent outbreak of the zombie virus
been taken to the court of European Rights today. After a long
hearing and a thorough examination of all evidence it has been
ruled that there is no indication that zombies are dangerous and
imprisonment of the dead is unlawful. The court granted*

zombies limited citizenship. This is good news for the FreeZom Campaigners as all zombies are to be returned to their families as soon as possible,' the reporter said.

'It's a trap,' said Mum. 'They are hoping we'll let out our relatives again so they can round them up.'

'Shush. I'm trying to hear this,' I said, then ducked as Mum automatically swung her arm to give me a clout.

'Furthermore the court ruled that any attempt to smash in a zombie's head will be considered assault.'

At that moment the camera switched to a group of protestors. Ms Havers jumped forward and grabbed the microphone from the reporter's hand. 'We at ZADPATEY believe that zombies are evil. Don't be fooled people. They are just waiting for an opportunity to EAT YOUR BRAINS!'

The reporter pulled his microphone away and the police came forward to push Ms Havers and her followers back.

'Lock your doors. Don't go out until this plague is destroyed.' yelled Ms Havers. 'I implore you … hit your dead over the head before they make a meal of you.'

'Brains?' said Granny as she sat down before the telly again. 'I'm a vegetarian…'

I looked at Mum and she squirmed a bit but didn't say anything. It wasn't usual these days for Granny to make much comment, but she was clearly still following what was happening in the world.

'Want some stout, Granny?' I asked later but she was zonked out in the chair, feet stretched out towards the telly.

The living room was freezing cold. We were wrapped up in sweaters and coats because we couldn't put the heating on.

'Mum?' I said later. 'What are we going to do if she

starts to smell a bit?'

'I don't know,' said mum. 'I'm trying to preserve her as best as I can. But I never thought I'd have this problem, always thought I'd shove her in a home when she got on my nerves too much. But I like her much better since she became a zombie. She's far less trouble.'

After a few weeks, the madness calmed down and the dead returned to the streets once more. As I went past the local burial service I noticed they had a new sign up. Last week they'd announced redundancies and closures since no one was burying their dead anymore. But now, there was a sign saying, GET YOUR DEAD EMBALMED TODAY.

When I got home, I noticed Granny was looking rather well. Her hair was brushed, false teeth polished and her skin had taken on a healthy glow.

'Get you,' I said.

'Been embalmed,' she mumbled, and then she sat down and pressed the remote control.

'Nice one,' I said.

'Will you take her out for a walk?' Mum asked later. 'She does so love to walk, but I don't like to let her out alone as she still hasn't learnt her way back home.'

A few minutes later we were shuffling proudly through the streets as Granny was showing off her new look to the other zombies.

'That looks good. Wonder if my wife will let me be embalmed,' said the butcher.

'Go home and ask her,' I suggested.

'Can't,' he said shaking his head sadly. 'Don't know the way.'

Luckily I remembered that they lived above his shop and Granny and I took him home. On the way back we helped a few more lost zombies.

'They really should wear address labels...' I said to Mum when we got back home.

Granny was really perky after the walk and we all played a game of scrabble. Of course her spelling was rubbish but Mum and I accepted her versions of words without argument. It was nice to be doing something so normal with her again.

The next day at school I joined Gemma and Billy in the canteen.

'The way I see it, there's a need for a service in this community. I've got an idea if you two fancy earning some money with me,' I said. 'Let's set up a walking service.'

'Urgh! I hate dogs,' said Gemma.

'I don't mean a *dog* walking service – I mean zombies.'

Billy started to laugh, almost choking on his beef sandwich, 'You're joking right?'

'I think that's a great idea,' said Gemma. 'I like the dead. We could all do with the extra money; and it's kind, as well. How do you think we should do this?'

I explained my plan and later that day in art, we made a poster advertising our services, and then photocopied it in the staff room while the teachers were outside smoking behind the bike sheds. On the way home we attached posters to lamp posts and walls.

It wasn't long before our service was taken up by locals with wandering dead relatives. We soon had a regular client list, and it stopped the random walking that had scared so many people. We discovered that walking the dead made them feel much better. It restored some of their basic thought and motor skills. It was why they liked to go out and walk around so much. It made them feel more alive again.

Within a few months Gemma, Billy and I had too

much work on our hands so we roped in a few more kids.

'I don't know how you can do it,' yelled Ms Havers as we passed her on the street.

We ignored her. She was just scum to us. After all she had an ASBO and a restraining order to keep her away from all zombies. I believed it was the only thing stopping her from whacking as many on the head as she could.

'It's people like you that give education a bad name,' Billy shouted as all three of us walked past her. She was always hanging around the off licence, now, holding a bottle in a brown paper bag. Her hair was wild, clothes unwashed and she looked more dangerous to us than our zombie clients ever could have.

When I got home that night I found Mum and Granny sitting together in the lounge.

'I finally found something she likes to drink,' said Mum and for the first time in ages she looked truly excited. 'I picked up a supply of embalming fluid to top her up and found her slurping from the jar through a straw.'

'It's good shit this stuff,' said Granny. 'Wanna try some?'

'No, thanks. Don't think it would agree with me. Maybe in a few years time when I'm a zombie.'

'Just hope she doesn't start peeing in the bed again,' Mum said. 'I'd never get that yellow stain out of the sheets.'

It didn't take long for a few more zombies to realise that drinking embalming fluid was fun and it gave them energy.

After that the zombies founded their own bars and clubs. You could see them sitting in roadside cafes drinking yellow gloop from fancy china. Granny joined a zombie group that met once a week and she regained a whole new lease on life. After all, she may have been dead and old but she no longer suffered from the aches and pains she once had before she died. She was, in fact, quite spritely these days.

It just goes to show you though; it all could have turned out so differently if we had listened to Ms Havers. My mum says it's George Romero's fault that we all thought the worst. Sometimes the cinemas show re-runs of the movies – they are all considered comedies and the zombies attend them in droves laughing at the absurdity.

'Why on earth would we want to eat brains,' said the butcher, 'when embalming fluid is so very, very good?'

I took the bag containing mum's meat order and paid him with my hard earned 'walking money'.

Billy, Gemma and I gave up school to run our Walking the Dead business. There really wasn't much point in continuing our education when we had a sure career already established, one that wasn't going to run out of clients anytime soon. Besides, the authorities were too busy arguing about the zombies to worry about a bunch of kids bunking off school.

There are still debates on telly about the ever-growing zombie population. Mum says the discussions will go on for ages, but I don't care about that. They've had a bad press for years. Some people say there's been a strange twist of fate, and that the zombies have turned out to be our future and shouldn't be feared. Mum says the jury's still out on that. But until someone proves otherwise I'll go on walking the dead.

SAM STONE began her professional writing career in 2007 when her first novel won the Silver Award for Best Novel with *ForeWord*

Magazine Book of the Year Awards. She is an award winning prolific writer of genre fiction. Her main passion is horror but her works are often mixed with other genres. She currently has two successful series: *The Vampire Gene* (hi-tech time-travelling vampire series), *The Kat Lightfoot Mysteries* (steampunk horror mystery series) and a science fiction fantasy trilogy called *The Jinx Chronicles*.

Since becoming a professional full time writer in 2008, Sam has written over 40 short stories, 15 novels, four novellas, audios, three screenplays (one due for DVD release in November 2017 the other two in pre-production) and a stage play. She has even written two official Sherlock Holmes stories for Constable and Robinson and Titan Books.

Stone is a regular guest at comic cons and conventions in the UK, USA and Canada and is very proactive in the genre community. She often delivers writing workshops at schools, colleges and theatres.

Stone currently resides in Lincolnshire with her husband David and cat Leeloo.

Visit www.sam-stone.com for more information.

LIFE IN A NORTHERN TOWN

Steve Lockley

Jack pressed himself tight into the recess in the wall and held his breath. The brickwork felt cold and damp against his back, even through several layers of clothes. He had made his bed there for the last few nights, sharing the space with other boys in the same position as he was; homeless and orphaned. Except he had a father somewhere even though he had not seen him for longer than he could remember. He still wore his father's scarf though, given to him when he had left to find work. There were times when he breathed deeply through the wool and thought he could still smell him on it.

Jack's mother had died three months ago and within days he had found himself on the streets, hoping to earn a few coins every day, but work was scarce. Even in the mills where the cotton fibres fell thick as snow and slowly filled the chests of the men and women who worked there until they could hardly breathe. Jack had worked in enough places like that to know the dangers of scrambling beneath the looms to recover dropped shuttles, or freeing a jammed mechanism, but even the chance of steady work like that relied on one of the existing workers of his own age to suffer an injury or be so ill they were unable to work. There had been times when he had felt so desperate he had wished that for an instant before the voice of his mother came to him from somewhere in the back of his mind, rebuking him for such a thought. Instead he had become part of a gang of twenty or so boys who looked out for each other, sharing food so that none of them should starve. Autumn had given way to winter, and soon it would be even more difficult to survive.

From somewhere in the press of small bodies he could he hear the sound of someone crying and another boy trying to offer comfort and muffle the sobs. It was the same every night, with at least one boy finding it hard to cope with the hand that life had dealt them. Jack had become outwardly hardened to it, but there were times in the middle of the night when he fought to hold back the sobs himself.

The last sounds of clogs on cobbles had long since faded and the clock in the square had sounded midnight. It would be another long night. The sky was clear and the full moon cast shadows in the graveyard beside the church. The porch did not feel like the most comforting place to be on a night like this but at least they would be left alone. More than once he had spent the night away from a town, out on the moors and quiet tracks that led from one place to another and he knew they were more dangerous places than this. He would rather risk the wrath of a man with a stick than a beast with teeth sharp enough to tear through flesh no matter what its size.

As the last echo of the one o'clock chime faded away Jack heard a sound that he had never heard in the town: the howl of a great beast. The other boys were roused in an instant and even in the dim light he could see the panic in their eyes. He had no idea why they should look to him, he was neither the leader nor the eldest, but Dan Samson was inclined to lash out at anyone who dared to disturb him and at that moment the lump lay unmoving on the single bench.

'What was that?' One of them asked in a whisper. It was impossible to tell which of the boys it was but it held the same fear that Jack was feeling himself.

'A bear,' one of the boys suggested.

'There aren't any bears in England,' Jack said.

'There are. I saw one once at the Goose Fair in Nottingham.'

'Maybe, but it wasn't running wild was it? Besides, bears don't howl like that. It sounded more like a dog.'

'Or a wolf,' another voice suggested.

'A wolf?'

'Are there any wolves around here?'

Jack had heard the stories about the wolf that had been seen out on the moors and fells, but no-one thought that a creature like that would come close to a town. Things like that killed for food and there were enough sheep out there to sate its appetite. There had to be. And yet he could not help but think that it might just be that creature they could hear now. The beast howled again and they clung together, all except Dan Samson who still lay unstirring oblivious to their fear.

No-one answered the question and they all seemed to be holding their breath, waiting for the second sound to break the night. When it finally came they could hold it no longer and it was all they could do to stop the boy they only knew as Worm from crying out. Jack suspected he was the one who had been crying in the night; it was usually him. Worm was the youngest and frailest of them and Jack already feared for what might become of him if there was a hard winter and they had not been able to find regular shelter by then. But at that moment the howling in the night worried him more than the fear of winter nights that sent a cold shiver up his spine.

A shadow moved in front of the row of houses opposite and Jack held his breath again, praying that everyone would remain still, even though he dared not make a sound. Samson let out a sudden snore, shifted and slipped off the bench he had been sleeping on while the boys around him tried to keep him quiet. The shape stopped moving and turned in their direction, two red pinpricks glowing in the darkness. Samson pushed two other boys off him and shouted out, outraged that they had tried to pin him down and the lights started to move towards them. It moved slowly at first, almost tentatively, but then they blinked and the shape moved faster until the darkness was closing the distance between them faster than any dog should have been able to.

Fear drove some of the boys into a run while it caused others to freeze. Samson was still struggling to come to terms with being woken from his sleep and clearly couldn't understand what was going on. Jack grabbed Worm and snatched him out of harm's way but there was nothing more he could do to help Samson. He knew that the larger boy would have done nothing to help the others if he had been the one to see the threat but that did not mean that he wished upon him the fate that was about to be delivered to him.

Claws snatched and silenced the boy's scream before it reached his lips and teeth tore at flesh. The creature gave out a howl but it was not the same as the one Jack had heard before, this was a cry of triumph and yet the prey had not been difficult to take. The beast feasted on the boy until blood no longer flowed freely from severed veins and arteries, but the other boys ran and the blood in their bodies pumped through vessels and organs faster than they had ever done before. There was no doubt that they were the lucky ones. They were the ones who would live to see another day.

Boys huddled behind gravestones, hoping they would not be seen, while others ran in the open, desperately trying to put as much distance as they could between themselves and the beast. But they should not have looked back, none of them. If they had kept going they would not have seen the sight that would haunt their dreams and nightmares for as long as they lived.

Jack struggled to get Worm to run, it was as if terror had gripped him and caused his legs to stop working. He was already convinced that the beast would not be satisfied with just one victim, it was behaving like a fox in a hen house that was caught up in the blood lust, killing every chicken for the sake of killing. The beast leapt at one of the boys still lurking in the churchyard, ripping at his flesh then dropping the frail body to the ground, casting a dark stain on the grass where the last of the bodily fluids seeped away. But it was enough, the beast was sated and after letting out another howl it sprang away from the body and ran away on all fours, covering the ground faster than anything Jack had ever seen before.

'Inside, quickly,' someone called from an open doorway and gradually the boys still close to the church moved towards the candlelight. Jack half carried Worm who was still struggling to regain control over his limbs. They had to walk closer to the second corpse than either of them wanted to but the danger of remaining out in the open longer by making a detour to skirt around it felt like a less palatable option.

Boys hurried inside one after another and two bolts were drawn into place once the last of them had crossed the threshold. The old man who had let them in placed the candle on the table and looked around at them all. It was a poorly furnished room but warm: a single armchair standing beside fireplace where embers still glowed in the grate. The man added kindling until it burst into life again them added more wood. Jack felt the heat coming from it quickly and the boys huddled around. None of them said anything for a while; each of them did nothing more than watch the flames dance across the log the man had placed in the grate.

'It's back then,' the man said at last, not taking his eyes from the fire. Old Tom kept the brazier burning outside the mill to give a few moments of warmth to anyone who wanted them.

'It's been here before?' Jack asked. He had not expected to hear anything like this.

'Years ago,' Tom said. 'It was here years ago.'

'But it went away?' All eyes were on the man as he pushed the poker into the fire, sending a shower of sparks up the chimney.

The man shrugged. 'Eventually. Once people learned to stay indoors after dark and keep the windows closed and doors bolted the killings stopped. I'm surprised that none of you remember.' He looked around at the faces lit by the firelight then added, 'I guess you are too young. Didn't your parents tell you about it?'

None of the boys responded and all stared into the fire with a far away look in their eyes rather than let Old Tom see the tears that were starting to well up in their eyes. In the end they did not have to say anything as Tom must have realised what he had said; none of these children had parents to warn them of the dangers that lurked in the dark.

'You'd better stay here tonight,' he said getting out of his chair. 'We'll see what we can do tomorrow to find somewhere you can be safe, at least until this thing has moved on somewhere else.'

Jack huddled down, holding Worm to him, the boy still silent and trembling. He spent the whole night watching the fire slowly die away until it was little more than glowing embers amongst the ash. They were safe for now at least, but it was impossible to know what the morning would bring.

Jack was the first to venture to the door at first light and open it a crack. Even with that limited view he could see one of the bodies, giving confirmation, as if any was needed, that it had been no dream.

'Come away,' Tom said gently, placing a hand on his shoulder and pulling him away from the door, closing it softly. 'People need to be told what happened if they didn't see it for themselves. Best if you all wait here for a little while. Let your friends sleep as long as they can.'

Jack took the chance to count the number of heads that were huddled in front of the fireplace. Some were sitting up and leaning against each other, while others had chosen to curl up in a ball. He counted seven including himself but there had been at least a dozen of them gathered together outside the church. He had seen the beast attack and kill two of them and could only hope that the others had been able to find somewhere else to hide. He feared for them though and knew that the streets of the town were no longer safe at night.

By the time the man returned some of the boys had

already chosen to leave. The events of the night before had scarred them and those felt they had any kind of alternative to the life they were leading, no matter how hard that might be; it was likely to be better than the risk of remaining. Jack was not sure if he even noticed that there were fewer boys in his front room when he returned than when he had left.

'The Priest is going to open up the church tonight so that you have somewhere to sleep safely at least.'

'How long do you think it will be before it's safe? Before it moves on?'

'Last time it was only three days, but we did not act quickly enough. We lost too many before it moved on to some other town.'

'Do you know where it went?'

'We heard from a few towns across the county that there had been trouble, but some kept tight lipped and denied anything had happened. No-one wants this thing, but nobody is going to try to kill it either.'

'And that's the best we can do? Hope that it will kill the people in another town instead of here. That just doesn't seem right. There must be a way of trying to stop it. Don't you have guns?'

'Not many, not here in the town. There's no call for them. '

'You have to find them from somewhere. We can't do nothing at all.'

'People aren't going to listen to me now are they lad. Not to old Tom Parsons. I'm just a mill hand, nothing more.'

'But you, you've found us somewhere to sleep.'

'There's one thing showing someone what his Christian duty is, and another to ask a man to put his life at risk. People remember what happened before.'

'But they've got to believe it. They can see with their own eyes what it did last night!'

'The bodies of those poor boys will have been cleared away long before the people of any importance get to hear about it.'

'But they need to see it. They need to understand how dangerous this thing is.'

'It doesn't work like that though does it? We don't get to tell the toffs what they are supposed to be thinking, what they are supposed to do. We are just hands, that's how they look at us. We are just part of the machinery. And if a few of us die, or are hurt, we can be replaced just like they would replace any other broken part of a machine.'

'It would be different if one of them had been killed you mean? If the animal had ripped the throat out of a toff's son instead of some homeless kids with no family to even miss them?'

The man didn't say anything but Jack knew that what he was saying was true. It would make all the difference in the world.

The church bell rang and doors opened along the street as people looked out tentatively while net curtains twitched in the houses of those too wary to allow even the morning air inside. Jack knew that most of them had been aware of what had happened the previous night, but no-one else had come to their rescue. They would rather watch children die than put their own lives at risk. They only cared about their own safety.

'Can you look after him?' Jack asked Tom, and the pair of them watched the small shape of Worm shift backwards and forwards.

'I wish I could, but there's only me.'

Jack held back what he was really thinking. It was one

thing for him to be outside taking his chances, but something had happened to Worm last night and who knew what might happen if he came face to face the creature again. One glimpse of the beast and what it was capable of doing had done this to him again and Jack couldn't let him go through it again.

'The vicar will make sure that there will be a place for both of you in the church tonight. The doors there are bigger and stronger than this. It might not be warm in there, but you will be safe at least.'

'Come on Worm. Looks like we're not wanted here,' Jack said churlishly, regretting the words the moment they had left his lips. There was every chance that Tom had saved their lives and the least he owed him was a little gratitude. He should have just said thank you and walked away but something made him want more.

The bodies were already being moved when they made their way back into the crisp morning air. Worm hung close to Jack, rarely more than a breath away from him. A couple of the other boys were standing around watching as the priest supervised the removal, having the bodies moved inside the church. In a town like this the dead would be laid out in their own homes until a funeral could take place, but these boys had no homes. The ground was iron hard with the heavy frost and it was difficult to imagine anyone being able to dig a hole deep enough to bury one, let alone two boys.

Dressed in his vestments the priest looked a strange figure amongst the bodies that had been destroyed in such a brutal way. Jack had seen him before many times, but the man had rarely acknowledged his existence. He knew that there were churches where even the porch was strictly out of bounds for boys without a roof over their heads. This one at least was happy to pretend that they did not exist, and if they did not exist their presence could be ignored. He could not ignore them now though; he would have to make choices that would decide their fate. If Tom was right and he would keep the church open to them then at least they would be safe. As the bodies were carried inside, Jack and Worm followed, not knowing where else they should go. The hunger was gnawing in their bellies but they could not even think about that. Not yet.

Inside, the church was cold and dark, early light struggling to break through the stained glass windows, but Jack suspected that it was always cold even in the height of summer. He watched as the bodies were laid out on the floor in front of the altar like some kind of offering. The bodies were stiff but he had no way of knowing if that was the stiffness of death or they were frozen solid. Either way he did not wish to get any closer to them than he already was.

Contented that the corpses had been dealt with to his satisfaction, the priest made his way to where Jack and Worm had taken a seat in the pews. Worm had curled up again and was already struggling to stay awake. Jack knew that it would be better for him if he could sleep, and if he could sleep it meant that he felt safe. Jack was not so sure.

'Were you with them?' The priest asked. There was no need for him to point to the bodies; they both knew only too well who he was talking about. Jack nodded.

'Did you see what did this to them?'

Jack nodded again.

'Can you describe it?'

'It was a great beast,' he said. 'With great jaws and sharp teeth. It was like a big dog, or maybe a wolf. But it was too big.'

'As big as a man?'

Jack thought about it for a moment. The beast had moved quickly, its motion often blurred and he had not wanted to look at it. He remembered the way that it had attacked the others, the screams as boys had run without any idea of where they were running to. Hot tears welled up and stung his eyes. He nodded and wiped them away. The priest put a hand on his head but it didn't make him feel any better.

'We have to stop it,' Jack said.

'No my son. This demon will be gone soon enough. You will be safe in here tonight. Have you eaten?'

Jack shook his head, but he wasn't really listening when the priest said that he would be back with food in a little while.

'In the meantime, if you see any of your friends they are welcome to stay here tonight, or as many nights as it takes.'

Jack nodded again. He heard the words, he would look for the others, but responding was not easy. He could not take his eyes from the two bodies lying on the ground, covered with white sheets, knowing what they were like beneath. Worm twitched in his sleep but at least they were dreams not nightmares. They would come soon enough.

The day passed slowly and gradually a few of the boys heard the message that they would be safe in the church, and that just as importantly that they would be fed, but not all of them stayed. People came and went; more interested in looking at the bodies than caring for the survivors, but most of them brought a small amount of food. Times were tight enough and he wondered how many of them could spare much more than the amount they gave. Jack knew that for him and the other boys, this would be the equivalent of a feast. But was it right that such a big price had been paid to get it?

By the time night fell, there was a growing sense of unease amongst the boys, they were torn between sitting at the front of the church, as far as they could possibly be from the great oak doors which would be locked as soon as the priest left, but not too close to the corpses lying on the cold stone floor. The priest had wanted to lock the door behind him taking the key with him. He had said that it was to ensure their safety, but Jack knew he was more concerned about what might be stolen if the building was not secured. He had no need to worry; none of them would want to leave the church while there was even a chance that the beast was out there. No-one in the building that night was going to be prepared to take the chance.

'I could stay if you want me to,' the priest said. It was an offer he was clearly hoping they would not accept. Jack knew that he would rather be in his own bed, safe behind his locked door with a fire roaring in the grate. He also knew that no-one would sleep that night no matter how warm and comfortable they were. Apart perhaps from the people in the big houses on the hill who kept themselves away from the poor, the needy, and the dead. Jack doubted that they even knew what had happened to the boys covered in sheets. And if they did, it seemed unlikely that they cared. They were just another couple of urchin boys. Two less mouths for society to feed.

There were only four of them sitting in the candlelight when the doors were slammed closed, others choosing to take their chances elsewhere, the draught causing the flames to gutter for a moment then return to life. Jack tugged on the handle to make sure that it was secure.

Even as he placed a hand on the door he felt his heartbeat increase as if it brought him closer to the beast. He lifted the scarf to his nose and breathed in deeply, hoping to catch his father's scent, even that would make it feel as if he was close; as if he was watching over him.

'It's going to be a long night,' he said to the other boys, there was a faint murmuring but no-one responded directly. Worm was still curled up on one of the pews, covered in one of the blankets the priest had supplied. He had been sleeping fitfully, at times crying out but never waking. Jack was worried about him but knew there was nothing he could do that would make him better. He would let him sleep for as long as he was able to, it would be better that way

'Do you really think we are safe in here?' one of the boys asked eventually. This was not the first time the question had been raised, and Jack suspected that it would not be the last before morning came around. 'It really can't get in, can it? Not in here? He wasn't lying to us.'

There was fear in the boy's voice and Jack did the best he could to reassure him. He could think of no place where they would be safer than they were at that moment. The thick stone walls and stout wooden door would keep an army at bay and the stained glass windows were set too high in the walls for any creature to come crashing through.

After eating their fill of the provisions that the townsfolk had left as an offering, they made themselves as comfortable as they could, settling down for a night when only Worm was likely to sleep. Cloud must have moved across the sky and cleared the path for moonlight to light up the stained glass window and Jack lay on the pew trying to make out what it was meant to represent.

He tilted his head to one side to see if that made it easier to make out, and although the shape suggested something he was not sure what it was. He kept the blanket wrapped tight around him and moved closer to the window to get a better look. He stared at the glass for a moment until he was sure what he could see and even when he did he remained motionless for another minute, making sure he took the whole scene in. The window showed a great beast, a creature that seemed to be half man half wolf. But the window was old which meant that the creature, or at least one like it, had plagued the village for a long time. It was no wonder that the adults were prepared for this, even if it had caught them unexpectedly

Worm cried out, but this was not the sudden panic of a nightmare, it was a cry of pain. He threw off the blanket he had been wrapped in for most of the day and shuffled into the aisle.

'Worm? Are you OK?' Jack asked but no clear sounds could find their way out of Worm's mouth. Jack moved towards him, seeing for the first time a dark patch in his side. Had he been hurt somehow? Worm let out another cry that was almost a scream and fell to the ground clutching his sides. Jack ran to him but as he closed the gap Worm raised his head and gave out a vicious snarl. Saliva frothed at his mouth which opened far wider than it was supposed to do. The small boy leapt at him, his hands outstretched like claws snatching at Jack's face, but Jack managed to slip to one side and Worm crashed into the end of a pew, releasing a howl of pain. The other boys were on their feet but they were only concerned with their own safety. The beast was inside with them; the beast was inside Worm. Instead of being safe they were caught like rats in a trap. Jack had to get out, not just to save himself but also to give the other boys a chance

If the others were intent on self preservation then it was going to be hard to subdue Worm. He may have been smaller than Jack but he had found a strength that he had not possessed before. Something had changed in him and this was not the boy he knew. This was not the same boy he had suffered the cold and damp with and shared the pangs of hunger.

Jack ran to the door, but the moment he was stationary he felt Worm springing towards him again. Claws snagged in his blanket and Worm crashed into the oak door, falling to the floor with the breath knocked out of him. Jack turned the key, but could not open the door as the weight of Worm's body was keeping it closed.

'Help!' He shouted as he struggled to prize the door open, shifting the prone body little by little, unwilling to touch it, but the other boys failed to come to his assistance. If he was going to get out he would have to do it without their help. Worm stirred, coming back to his senses, and started to get to his feet, allowing Jack to open the door another fraction. But it was not enough. He needed a weapon to try to defend himself, at least to hold the beast at arm's length, but there was nothing obvious that would do the job. As he stepped backwards the door burst open with enough force to send Worm staggering away from it, howling with pain. Jack thought someone had heard the noise and come to their aid, but his heart sank when he saw that the newcomer was not Tom, their saviour from the previous night, not even the priest who had given them shelter in his church, but the great beast who had killed the two boys who lay only yards away. The beast that had without doubt caused the change in Worm.

Worm lay whimpering on the floor as the beast moved slowly towards Jack. Its great jaws slavered, tongue lolling from one side of its mouth. There was no running away, no chance of escape. Jack fell to his knees, closed his eyes and clasped his hands together. His dry lips searched for the words of a prayer, feeling that there was nothing left he could do. He felt the creature's hot breath upon him but mixed in with it was a familiar smell that almost gave him hope and stopped him being afraid. He waited for the blow that would end his life but it did not come. There was another howl and when he opened his eyes he saw the beast leaving the church, dragging Worm behind him.

The two other boys ran the length of the church, gaining courage now that the danger was gone, and slammed the door behind the monsters and turned the key in the lock once more. They stood looking down at Jack where he was still kneeling, still clasping his hands together in prayer. He thought for a moment that his prayers had been answered, that God had come to his rescue. But then he remembered the familiar smell in the beast's odour, knowing that somehow it had helped him conquer his fear. Then he breathed through his father's scarf again and he knew.

STEVE LOCKLEY is the author of around a hundred short stories, including contributions to a couple of *Doctor Who* anthologies. Many of his collaborations with Paul Lewis have been pulled together in the collection, *The Winter Hunt And Other Stories.*

His most recent novel is *The Empty Desk,* featuring the characters from the popular TV series, *Ghost Whisperer*.

Steve also works as a freelance editor and has served as a judge for the World Fantasy Awards.

He's delighted to have been asked back to the SciFi Weekender!

HOLLOW

Simon Morden

Jo dreamt that she was dying, and when she woke up it seemed to be true. Metal bulkheads screamed, rivets popped and howled like bullets, the whole rig shuddered with fear and trembling. Perpetual lights flickered and died, and in the shadows, something strong and glistening erupted through the floor of her cabin.

Her scream joined the sparking shriek of friction, and she shrank into the corner of her bunk. Her bare knees drew up reflexively to protect her body, and her thin hands went over her head.

The darkness was grudgingly replaced by sickly green emergency illumination. Echoing concussions rattled the superstructure. In her panic they sounded like explosions, and only when the door to her cabin was thrown open did she realise that they were running feet.

A torch beam skittered over her white face.

'Jo? Jo! You okay?'

'What the hell is that?' she managed before her voice failed.

The man shone his torch from the floor where the rubber matting had peeled open like a flower, to the ceiling where the steel tube had punched through to the level above. It was wet with mud and seawater. 'Part of the drill string. It's all over the rig.'

Jo shook her head to clear the fog inside it. 'Matthew?' She'd had a brief fumbling encounter with the engineer in the mud-logging shack, which she had instigated, then terminated. She covered her naked legs with a blanket.

He looked away, his mouth a thin line within his full black beard. 'I just wanted to make sure you weren't hurt. I've got to check the rest of the corridor.'

'I'm fine. Shocked but fine.'

'Get into your survival suit and get to muster stations. I don't know how bad this is.' Matthew and his unseen colleague backed out, leaving the door open.

She found a pair of canvas trousers and dragged them on, tucking her night-shirt into the waistband. Her work boots were under her bunk, with her socks still balled in the top. The giant orange survival suit was in her locker, three doors down on the right: the company had drilled her until she could put it on blind.

Before she left her room, she reached out a tentative hand and touched the drill casing turned impromptu pillar. Moments before it had been hundreds of feet below her feet, buried in the rock of the Atlantic continental shelf. Matthew might not know how bad it was, but Jo did.

She waddled out onto the deck, unprepared for the low ruddy sunlight that made her squint. The sun was broaching the north-east horizon, revealing a rig in chaos. Angles had changed. There were pieces of metal in unfamiliar locations, and great holes gouged in walls and floors, as if they'd taken the brunt of an artillery exchange.

Jo avoided grabbing for a missing section of handrail, deciding that going overboard was not wise. She was the only woman in a crew of seventy, and she had no doubt that every last one of them would dive in to save her, the chauvinist fools.

At the end of the gantry was her muster station, next to one of the free-fall red lifeboats. The company had made her practice that, too, and she swore she was an inch shorter because of it. As she joined the crowd, the muster officer ticked his list.

'The Chief wants to see you on the Bridge.' His tone was guardedly neutral, and she wondered what she'd done wrong. Her mind raced. It was her first offshore job, and if this mess was her fault, it was going to be her last.

'Now?' It was a stupid response, but it was all she could think of. She had already turned to the stairs up to the drilling deck before a withering reply could be aimed at her.

The stacks of unused casing were scattered like jackstraws: Jo's short legs weren't going to negotiate the deck without disappearing into the maze of pipes. It was unnecessarily dangerous, and she didn't have to go that way. She climbed down again, passed the accusing stare of the muster officer, and did a stumbling run to the far corner of the lower deck. The stairs there ran straight up to the Bridge. She arrived, sweating from exertion and nerves, her face red and her lungs labouring.

'What the hell happened?'

It wasn't the greeting she expected, especially from the Old Man himself. He knew everything.

'I don't know. What did happen?' She closed the outside door and weaved her way around the plotting table. The Chief stood with his back to the picture window, leaning against the dulled radar console.

'The drill string came back up like it'd been fired from a cannon. I've four men dead, and another six so badly hurt the Doc's wondering if he can keep them alive long enough for them to become someone else's problem.'

Her hand went to her mouth. 'Dead?'

'How did this happen?' The Chief didn't do rhetorical questions. He wanted an answer.

And at that moment, Jo forgot everything she knew about geology. She couldn't even remember when the Jurassic was, let alone the foraminifera about which she was supposed to be an expert. She stalled. 'What about the blow-out preventer?'

'The whole stack, all four tons of it, went through the engine room like a fist. We're on emergency generators, we've lost six of eight anchors, we're dead in the water and we're sinking.' A telephone rang, and he snatched it up. 'Bridge.'

He listened for a moment, then launched the handset back down into its cradle. He turned his broad back on her and stared out at the sea.

Jo took a deep breath. 'Blow-outs aren't this powerful. There was nothing in the well-log to predict this, nothing in seismics. We don't even know if there's oil down there.' Her voice trailed off, but she regained her composure. 'I'll go and check the readings again, but it's kind of too late, isn't it?'

'The port pontoon is holed and taking on water. We're having to deliberately fill the starboard one to compensate, or we'll turn turtle. I've called the *Petrel* alongside to start taking the crew off. I'm ordering everyone to abandon ship.' His shoulders slumped in defeat. 'This should never have happened.'

'You're blaming me,' she said.

'No. I'm blaming whatever that is.' The Chief pointed out of the window at a spot a hundred yards distant.

Jo walked slowly over and craned her neck. The surface of the slowly rolling sea was boiling. A broad circle of white foam, sharply delineated against the grey Atlantic, churned like it was on a stove.

'We were on station over that.'

Professional curiosity won out over self-interest. The Chief suggested that she be in the first helicopter across to the supply ship, because she was a woman and no other reason. She declined gracefully but firmly.

Instead, she got hold of a gas probe and held it out on its telescopic pole in the direction of the bubbling sea. It occurred to her that if there was a jet of methane off the starboard bow, it would only take a change in the wind direction to blow them all into orbit. The rig's own diesels, the helicopter, the supply ship, a stray scrape of metal on metal, would be all it would take to ignite the biggest flammable gas cloud in recorded history.

No matter how much she turned down the sensitivity of the machine, she couldn't register a single hydrocarbon. Neither could she detect a greater concentration of any single gas.

'Air,' she said to herself. 'We're leaking air.'

'What did you say?'

Jo jumped, and almost dropped the probe. It was a

long way down to the sea, though less than it ought to be. They were sinking, after all.

'Matthew.'

'The Chief wants you on the next flight.'

'Of course he does. He wanted me on the last one, too.' She stowed the probe and turned the machine off. 'I think it's a jet of air. Where it's coming from is anyone's guess.'

Matthew purposefully took the detector by its handle. 'The helideck?'

'When I'm ready. I want to get the hard drive from the computer in the shack. It's got everything on it.'

'I'll bring it with me.'

'No,' she said, suddenly angry. 'It's my bloody computer. I'll get it.' She watched the expression on his face go hard. 'You don't get to tell me what to do: you're not my boyfriend.'

'You've made that abundantly clear.'

'Go and do some engineering, Matthew. It's what they pay you for, not trying to nursemaid me.' She snatched the gas detector back and pretended to study the little crystal screen.

'Make sure you're on that next flight, or I'll carry you on myself.' When she gave him a furious stare, he laughed at her. 'Like I care.'

Jo felt she was going to cry: just like a girl, she thought, and gritted her teeth, willing the tears back in. 'Just go.'

When she was alone, she climbed up to the drilling deck. The door to her mudlogging shack was partially blocked by a stray section of casing. She tried to roll it away by bracing her back against a wall and heaving with both feet. It moved only enough to open the door a little, but it was sufficient to let her squeeze past, even with the bulk of her survival suit.

By touch, she unplugged the back of the computer from all its peripherals, and with a wry smile of satisfaction, she pushed the monitor off the top and heard it crack against the floor. All the geophysical information they'd collected was stored on the hard drive: the well logs, the seismic charts and the gravity surveys. If there was a reason for the catastrophic blow-out, it'd be somewhere amongst the data.

It'd be a reason she'd have to work out back on dry land, and not three hundred miles west of the Orkneys on a crippled semi-submersible rig.

A downdraught from the helideck riffled the loose pages on her desk. The chopping rotors of the helicopter rattled the air, and the door slammed shut, leaving her in total darkness. Jo swore under her breath and groped for the door handle. It turned, but wouldn't open.

She shouldered the door with all her tiny strength. A sliver of light showed around the frame. The pipe she'd moved to get in had slipped, trapping her.

Panic rose in her throat. She couldn't draw breath, and the sweat poured off her, plastering stray blonde hairs to her forehead. She struggled to get the tips of her fingers into the gap, and only succeeded in making her knuckles bleed.

She slumped down, her back to the door. Now that she had time to think, she turned on the torch attached to the breast pocket of her suit. Weak light filtered through the steel shelving, illuminating the maps and charts tacked to the walls.

She was a scientist. She knew what she had to do.

After twenty minutes of eye-straining work, she had unscrewed one of the shelving supports and slipped the box-sectioned column over the handle of her trusty five-pound geology hammer. She kicked the wedge of the hammer into the gap of the door, and heaved on her makeshift lever. Everything bent at once; the door and the shelving. The hammer, bless it and those who made it, hung on to do the job. The door was open wide enough to get her slim arm through, and consequently she could walk the obstructing pipe clear.

She worked methodically, relaxing into the rhythm of push and haul, push and haul. The deck was tilting towards her, and she had to chock the pipe every cycle, or it would roll back, eating up the ground so determinedly won. Eventually, she was able to brace the door with the hammer, slide the computer out onto the deck and slip out after it.

The helicopter lifted off from the helideck. For a fleeting moment, she could see the faces of the crew inside, swathed like her in their orange survival suits. Then it turned, dipped and roared away. The exhaust from the engine was briefly hot, then it was gone. One more round trip, and they'd all be off. The rig would sink gracefully in four hundred feet of water, and probably bankrupt some Lloyds Names in the process.

She retrieved her hammer, stuck in her belt for sentimental reasons, and picked up the computer case. The drilling deck was still a chaotic tangle of pipework, so she retraced her steps to the lower gantry, and worked her way around two sides of the rig. The sea was visibly closer, little white horses tipping each wave over as they washed around the supporting legs.

The *Petrel* was a wide white ship, converted from a North Sea ferry to trailing after exploration rigs. A helideck had been welded onto the aft, and there was a man dressed in yellow coveralls stood on it, waving two bright sticks of light to guide the aircraft in.

As Jo watched, a patch of ocean fifty yards across between the *Petrel* and the rig turned translucent. The rig shuddered and reared away, and Jo felt herself falling. It was either the computer or her: no choice, despite all the effort she'd expended in getting it. It went over the side and she darted out her hands to grab something, anything.

She connected with a storm rail and hung on. The rig was turning and tilting, caught in a current of immense power. The sea plumed like a whale broaching the surface, and boiled away, hissing and roaring with a furnace intensity.

She clung to the rail and tried to turn to see the *Petrel*. The helicopter was upside down, briefly, before the still-spinning rotor blades clawed at the inconstant sea. The *Petrel* itself was swallowed whole as another plume opened up beneath it. One moment, it was floating on the surface: the next, it was falling into the depths below like a stone. It disappeared, leaving a smoking slick of burning aviation fuel as a wreck marker.

The rig stabilised itself lower in the water. She stared at the black cloud torn by strange winds, and slowly got to her feet. She screamed herself hoarse. All hope of rescue had gone.

The remnant assembled on the bridge. There were fifteen of them, the senior crew who had stayed behind to supervise the evacuation of their sections.

The Chief was outwardly calm, but the shortness of his sentences and his temper betrayed his feelings.

'Mayday signal is on automatic. We've lost all

anchors. The nearest ship is thirty miles away, but it won't come close because of what happened to *Petrel*. Everything staying equal, we'll sink in two hours time. We're our own salvation, gentlemen. And lady.' He grimaced. 'Any suggestions?'

The toolpusher, a granite-faced Norwegian, turned to Jo, and asked her directly. 'What is going on down there?'

She cleared her throat, which hurt. Everyone was waiting for an explanation, something to call their enemy. 'There must be a reservoir of gas trapped in the rock. We've punctured it, and it's coming out at tremendous pressure, at least a kilobar. As the pressure inside the reservoir drops, the roof will start to collapse. It'll mean more jets, bigger each time until there's a catastrophic failure. All the remaining gas will rush to the surface, and there'll be an almighty tidal wave.' She blinked. 'That's just an educated guess. Take it or leave it.'

'So why did the *Petrel* sink?' persisted the toolpusher. 'Why so fast?'

'There was too much air in the water. The displacement of the *Petrel* dropped below its tonnage. It suddenly found itself flying. Where else could it go but down?' She shrugged. 'I could demonstrate with a glass, a cork and a straw, but that would be a bit pointless.'

'This collapse: when will it come?' asked Henry. He was a lean Australian, a diver by trade.

'It could already have started.' She watched the ripple of disapproval touch each face. 'Look: this has never happened before. They didn't teach me in rock school how to deal with the impossible. I'm making this up as I go along, and I don't hear any intelligent suggestions coming from you lot.'

'Enough.' The Chief slammed his hand down on the plotting table. 'One thing is clear,' he said into the silence, 'this is a unique situation that requires a unique solution. We seem to be sitting on top of a disaster, and the more we know about it, the better chance we have of living through it. I've seen most of my crew drown or burn this morning, and I've no intention of watching those left go the same way. Henry, can we still launch the remote sub?'

'Sure. It was charged and ready to go. How we get it into the water is a bit trickier. I don't know if any of the cranes are working.'

'We can make something happen,' said Matthew, in his capacity as First Engineer. 'Even if we have to lower it down by hand.'

'Get to it.'

Matthew, the Second Engineer and the Head Electrician left with Henry. The Chief unrolled a chart of their exploration block. 'Talk to me, Jo.'

She leant over the map, her finger tracing out the Rockall Rise and the Faeroes Trench. 'You can get great quantities of trapped gas in magma. About fifty million years ago, the Atlantic was forming. There were rift zones all around: between Greenland and Canada; between Britain and Ireland; before the one between Ireland and Greenland became dominant. Volcanic eruptions like they have on Iceland now.'

'We're over a newly active volcano? That doesn't sound good.'

'It depends. Once the gas has blown off, there'll be a partial collapse of the magma chamber. Things might quieten down for a bit. Of course, the geophysics doesn't show any of that, and we'll all be in the sea long before.' She hung her head and bit her lip. 'Chief? I'm sorry.'

The Chief scrubbed his cheeks. 'I've never lost a command in twenty-five years. But I'm losing this one, and there's not a damn thing I can do.'

The Electrician opened the Bridge door. 'We're ready to go.'

They crowded outside to watch. The lobster-like minisub was dangling from a cradle slung beneath one of the derrick cranes. Lars the toolpusher took his seat at the controls, and swung the arm out over the sea.

The sub disappeared over the edge of the rig, and they retreated back to the Bridge to watch the video screens. Henry waited until the sub entered the water before testing the systems. 'Lights. Cameras. Propulsion. Hydroplanes. Batteries are good. Let's see what we can see.' He released the locking ring, and submerged the craft.

He span it around the port pontoon. There was a collective indrawing of breath. The steel hull was speared by two sections of casing, from which streams of bubbles progressed inexorably upwards. There was far too much damage to effect a repair, even if they had had enough time.

Down and down, past blank-eyed fish and quick phosphorescent flashes, until the seabed glimmered into view. They were looking at bare rock.

Jo spoke first: 'Where's the sediment gone?'

'Current is pretty strong. Things are stirred up down there.' Henry was constantly adjusting the position of the sub with a flick of the joystick.

'But there should be at least a couple of feet of muck. It's been swept clean.'

'Let's go north-west and have a look at the first

plume.' By common consent, he steered the sub away from where the *Petrel* went down. The last thing they wanted to see were the faces of their drowned friends staring back at them through the video link.

As they approached, they skimmed the seabed. The screen showed scoured, striated rock, and a series of arcing steps going down.

'Surface fractures. It's already starting to go.'

Henry wasn't paying attention. 'Telemetry's gone wrong. We're losing control.'

The Chief stepped forward and scrutinised the flickering numbers on the screen. 'The sub's not moving. We are.' He turned to the window. The horizon was different. It seemed to be dented.

'I can't see what that is.' The only reference point they had, the plume they were investigating, slid clockwise. 'We're turning.'

As they watched in silence, a great bowl of spinning water crept into view. A mile-wide whirlpool, and they were in its grip.

Some ran for the lifeboats. Some sank to the floor and shrank in on themselves. Jo gazed in reverential awe. By putting her hands on the triple-thick glass, she could feel its power. She was the lint in an emptying bath, being swept away down the drain.

The whirlpool turned the rig around, and it dropped out of view. Released from its mesmerising grip, she picked her way over the legs of the fallen to the deserted minisub controls.

She steered the sub using the lights and the current. The dark sea on the screen slowly turned pearly white. She angled the sub's thrust to go with the spin of the whirlpool, watching the speed in knots pick up, faster and faster. When she was in the throat of the beast, she gave the electronic order to blow the sub's tanks.

It surfaced in a maelstrom of mist. As the sub flipped, she saw the rig, low in the water, surrounded by a standing wall of water. Then it turned over again, and fell into the funnel. The water was glassy green, torn and stretched, and the centre was luminous. Even when the tunnel went black around her, there was still light at the end.

'Look,' she heard herself saying. 'The Earth is hollow. There's another sun down there, another world, and we're drowning it all.'

No-one paid her any attention; they were trapped in their own catatonic fortresses.

The forces acting on the little sub overwhelmed it. The camera lens crazed and imploded. The numbers tumbling on the screen became a series of dashes. Far, far below her, a man-made object of metal and plastic plunged into an alien sky.

She stumbled out onto the deck. The roar of falling water was full and round, rendering speech impossible. The rig was spinning on its axis, and increasing speed with every revolution. The water was now up to the lower level where she had made the gas reading earlier. She watched the waves cover the lattice gantry, retreat, then overwhelm it.

Matthew was standing there. He looked up and raised his hand to her. He climbed over the submerged railing, and just let go.

It was tempting. She had no desire to die alone, but her fear of death was greater. The orange suit separated from the side. When the rig spun around again, he had gone.

The only place left to go was the drilling tower. The derrickman's platform was eighty feet up, waving around like a topsail in a gale. Despite the immediate danger presented by the chaotic casing-strewn deck, she picked her way over the shifting pipes, jumping from one to another as they slued and clanged together. She had to throw herself at the leg of the derrick, and hang on tight. The whole rig tilted, and groaned in pain. She was looking down the same route the minisub had taken, and it was infinitely more terrifying than on the small screen.

She climbed. Hand over hand, boots banged down on each rung to make sure of her footing, arms straining against the constantly changing forces acting on her. One moment she was pulled away, the next thrown against the ladder. Her hair was wringing wet with spray, and she was deaf with the noise.

She made the platform just as the water reached the base of the derrick. Whatever buoyancy the inundated pontoons had left disappeared. The sea rose to meet her, swiftly, inevitably. There was just time enough to pull the ripcord that inflated the suit. She was afloat, and between her feet, the derrick shrank away.

She lay back, arms spread wide. Her body bowed as it hovered on the shoulder of the funnel, then she was over. Mind numb, eyes unblinking, she began her descent.

For her, there was no light to aim for: the way to the inner world was sealing even as she went to greet it. The dark heart of the whirlpool swelled, and the ocean jerked and danced, spasming with discord. The whole great bowl of water went white with shock, and she felt it hard and real in her gut. Fountains punched the air, and there was no support for her anymore. She closed her mouth and wondered what it would be like to drown.

Her hair spread about her like a net in the deep blue sea, sparkling globes of air suspended about her, white diamonds against the dark. Finally, she could hold the breath in her lungs no more. With passing regret, she exhaled, and the world began to fade away. There was beauty, and there was peace. She was aware of her body being caught up, ascending from the deep on her way to shining Heaven.

She felt wind on her face, and sun on her eyelids. Without thinking, she drew breath, retched brine, and gasped again. She became aware that she was still alive. She laughed for laughter's sake: this was the release that came from cheating death, the calm and relief and thankfulness at being spared when everyone else had been claimed. Guilt would come only later, along with the nightmares and waking unease, the dread of open water that would take a lifetime of conquering.

A perfectly circular wave spread out across the Atlantic. At its focus was Jo, an orange speck in the wide, wide ocean.

Gateshead-based **DR SIMON MORDEN** trained as a planetary geologist, realised he was never going to get into space, and decided to write about it instead. His writing career includes an eclectic mix of short stories, novellas and novels which blend science fiction, fantasy and horror, a five-year stint as an editor for the British Science Fiction Association, a judge for the Arthur C Clarke Awards, and regular speaking engagements.

Simon has written eight novels and novellas. The wonderfully tentacular *Another War* (2005), was shortlisted for a World Fantasy Award, and 2007 saw the publication of *The Lost Art*, which was shortlisted for the Catalyst Award. The first three books starring everybody's favourite sweary Russian scientist, Samuil Petrovitch (*Equations of Life, Theories of Flight, Degrees of Freedom*) were published in three months of each other in 2011, and collectively won the Philip K Dick Award – the fourth Petrovitch, *The Curve of the Earth*, was published in 2013.

In a departure to the usual high-tech mayhem, 2014 saw the arrival of *Arcanum*, a massive (and epic) alternate-history fantasy.

Most recently published are the *Books of Down* (Gollancz), the first two being *Down Station* and *The White City* – set in a fantasy world where what you are is what you become, and chronicling the trials and triumphs of Down's latest refugees on the run from a disaster that might just have destroyed all of London.

COPYRIGHT INFORMATION

Other Telos Horror Titles

<u>DAVID J HOWE</u>
TALESPINNING

<u>FREDA WARRINGTON</u>
NIGHTS OF BLOOD WINE

<u>PAUL LEWIS</u>
SMALL GHOSTS

<u>STEVE LOCKLEY & PAUL LEWIS</u>
KING OF ALL THE DEAD

<u>SIMON MORDEN</u>
ANOTHER WAR

<u>SAM STONE</u>

THE VAMPIRE GENE SERIES
Horror, thriller, time-travel series.
1: KILLING KISS
2: FUTILE FLAME
3: DEMON DANCE
4: HATEFUL HEART
5: SILENT SAND
6: JADED JEWEL

JINX CHRONICLES
Hi-tech science fiction fantasy series
1: JINX TOWN
2: JINX MAGIC
3: JINX BOUND (Forthcoming)